I0846752

VENICE
NOIR

VENICE NOIR

GUIDO EEKHAUT

All rights reserved, including without limitation the right to reproduce this book or any portion thereof in any form or by any means, whether electronic or mechanical, now known or hereinafter invented, without the express written permission of the publisher.

This is a work of fiction. Names, characters, places, events, and incidents either are the product of the author's imagination or are used fictitiously. Any resemblance to actual persons, living or dead, businesses, companies, events, or locales is entirely coincidental.

Copyright © 2024 by Guido Eekhaut
Originally published as *Venezia Oscura* by Poespa Productions, Gent, Belgium, 2024.

ISBN: 979-8-3372-0262-4

This edition published in 2026 by Open Road Integrated Media, Inc.
180 Maiden Lane
New York, NY 10038
www.openroadmedia.com

VENICE
NOIR

1

Tourists don't come to Venice this late in the year—it's November after all—except to commit suicide in some disreputable hotel. They do this for reasons known only to them, mostly money or lost love, and often a fatal combination of both. Fortunately, the number of suicide tourists is relatively low, which alleviates the burden on local police and consulates. Neither police officials nor diplomats would find the trouble particularly enjoyable, especially when it requires them to visit various seedy hotels located in half-forgotten alleys.

This is not my first time in this stubborn and haughty Doge's City, but this time I am here on my own, in a situation with which even the extremely civilized young man occupying the reception desk of the Carlton Hotel seems to have a problem. Even though his face displays no emotion, I sense a moment of uncertainty. A woman traveling alone? He has never experienced such a perplexing situation before. He will of course remain polite, but only because I am a guest.

"Signora Barth . . ."

"And make that a suite," I continue, as casually as possible, after telling him that the room will be single occupancy, yes, with only one breakfast. "A suite would be a splendid idea. I like to enjoy the extra space."

British and American women, like me, accompanied Allied troops through the war zone that used to be Italy ten years ago, and not exactly in the rear guard. Most of us still bear the physical and emotional scars of our lust for action and danger. Why can't I then travel independently and spend the night in this luxurious five-star hotel? I can do it without a man's protection. But this attitude already guaranteed me problems in my own suffocating British homeland, and even more so in rigid Catholic Italy, where, even today, fascism proliferates in people's minds. Women have just as few rights in public life as they do in the Church.

"Of course, Signora," says the receptionist, a handsome boy of perhaps twenty. His name is Alberto, as his brass nameplate attests, an item which he probably polishes every evening and carefully places on his bedside table so he doesn't forget to wear it the next morning. His uniform is dove gray and white, with a black tie. Neat, all too neat. He is a function rather than a person. A photo in the hotel's catalog will likely identify him as the youngest but also the most dynamic employee. Maybe that alone will get him promoted next year. "A suite, then. We have an excellent suite on the, er, third floor, overlooking the Canale. However, there is a small additional charge. Everyone wants to look out at the Canale, is it not?"

I defyingly slap my Lloyds Bank checkbook on the counter, screw open my golden fountain pen, and he immediately knows that the small extra charge will be no problem, not even worth mentioning. This Signora not only travels alone; she is also able to immediately pay an advance in hard currency. Of course, the young man understands the significance of a checkbook from this specific bank. In a moment, he will offer me either the royal suite or (more probable) the presidential one, given that nearly all of these continental European countries have now become republics.

"A week, to start with," I say. A budding mustache grows between his lip and nose but still needs a lot of care. In the meantime, the bellboys will have taken my luggage from the private water taxi. It was cold on the canal just now, but I am wearing a sturdy woolen greatcoat of the kind that visiting ladies in this hotel rarely or never want to be seen in. Just wait until I put on my leather jacket. I also wear black cotton trousers and ankle boots. When I parade through the hotel foyer dressed like that, there will be frowns, but no one will stand in my way, mainly because of doubts about my social status. I don't fit into this community's scenario. The local population does not speak the language in which I tell my story.

The hotel's hall is rather modest in size, featuring a counter of café-au-lait-colored wood on the left, a floor of ivory-hued marble tiles with gold-colored divisions, and a vast salon with a glass roof. The furniture is at the same time dismissive and inviting, a bit like I would imagine Napoleon's salon to be. You'll find a collection of armchairs and sofas, adorned with taupe fabric and dirty silver armrests, here, while another collection, entirely in gold, is located elsewhere. Two deep niches in the walls house exuberant green plants. On one of the tables sits a small, simple vase with a single carnation, as well as a lonely, empty serving bowl made of expertly crafted silver. The other glass tables display international fashion magazines. No one could possibly feel at home in this setting.

I hand the check over to Alberto, who barely spares it a glance, as etiquette requires. The gold-plated key with the discreet dark red leather strap is now my property. The room number is an equally discreet steel plate glued to the leather. The luxury is in the details. It is also shrouded in silence.

My accommodation turns out to be as expected: spacious and overlooking the canal and jetties on the other side, as well as a building in classic palazzo style. That channel is more narrow than I expected. Its water is gray, and no fish might survive in it. I have a salon (two armchairs and a sofa, a bar cabinet with full bottles of Amaretto and cognac, and some other stuff), as well as a bedroom with a bed in which I can sleep two, maybe three lovers. Adjacent is a marble bathroom with both a shower and bath, a luxury that I am rarely granted even in my own country.

This is the true life. That is precisely why I returned to Italy.

Life has ever served me worse. Ten years ago, I sought refuge in ragged military tents, remnants of a past war, or, at most, in a ruined farm reeking of manure, or in a dusty and empty convent where nuns had suffered sexual abuse just a week before. I had to be constantly on the lookout for mines and snipers (German ones, mostly), for the grabby hands of American soldiers newly drafted from their parents' farm and still smelling of cow dung and soured milk, and for the vengeance of poorly shaven Italian fascists. Along with Polish, British, and Canadian soldiers, I experienced hunger and thirst, and like everyone else, I faced indiscriminate gunfire. I recall the ripe stench of decomposing corpses among the ruins of razed villages. Now, I find myself in the most beautiful city in this country, where rationing has long since ceased, unlike in my own not-so-great United Kingdom. There is even fresh fruit in a bowl on the sideboard.

Between these events and over the course of these ten years, life has been full of ups and downs, marked by both good and bad resolutions, betrayals, and worse. However, now that I am here, I can confidently say that it has all been worth it, despite the fact that some individuals can no longer recount their entire story. However, their suffering has disappeared deep into history's sewers, leaving no story intact.

Fresh flowers adorn the dresser in the salon. When two servants come in with my luggage and glance at me inquiringly, I tell them I want my stuff in the bedroom and reward each of them excessively with a five-pound note because I haven't had time yet to change my funds into lira. I realize the sum might be something like a week's wages here. I am pleased that I can make a positive impact on the local economy.

I'm also delighted I can spend my soon-to-be-former husband's family money, because that's what I do. They have plenty of funds, and they will pay for the injustice he did to me and for the unkind treatment I received from them over the past two years. They have come to understand this divorce, and specifically my discretion, will cost them a good deal of money. I am well aware of their shady business interests, and they know that I know, so my silence comes at a cost. It's a price expressed in brutally hard currency. That is why I can use Lloyds Bank as a shield against poverty. No bread or soup lines in the rain for me.

However, my greatest leverage against my former in-laws is of a particularly personal nature. I'll make no bones about it: I caught my husband being unfaithful to me. In itself, not really a major transgression in their midst, given the number of ancestors and living relatives who eagerly jumped into bed with someone not mentioned on their marriage certificate. If it all happened discreetly and more or less within the same social class, eyes would be averted and gossip muted, and sometimes those involved would simply be paid off. The sinful bed partners quickly disappeared from view, and children born out of passion were denied and ignored.

That's just part of upper-class life, isn't it?

In my husband's case, however, the problem was of a different nature. I caught him in bed with another man. I don't intend to be vindictive or narrow-minded, but this went a little too far where I am concerned.

That kind of intimate activity is not appreciated, certainly not in his circles. They are all prim and unyielding hypocrites, especially when it comes to sex. But even if they were to close ranks, there would be another and rather more pressing problem: homosexuality is a criminal offense in the United Kingdom. In addition, his partner appeared willing to make a statement before a judge to save himself. That's awful enough, if it weren't for the fact that my husband wrote him a number of passionate, revealing love letters. Letters that I have read when I came into possession of them. They made me blush on account of their daring language and their intimate outpourings. I was envious of them, as I had never received such passionate writing from him.

Naturally, I carefully stored those letters, understanding their intrinsic value. Reading his descriptions and feelings made me realize that I deserved a substantial financial reward. His family has already paid an advance. But I demand more. Much more. Those Venetian five-star hotels do not come cheap. Traveling around Europe in a way that suits me is equally expensive.

However, my presence in this city and at this time have nothing to do with my marital issues or conflict with my ex-in-laws. I'm here because of a strange and unusual letter, as well as a fascinating and attractive offer, the source of which remains unknown. Otherwise, I wouldn't have come to Venice this late in the year, preferring to relax on a beach in Crete or somewhere similar. With an exciting book. And lots of wine. And maybe even with a lover, but discreetly.

2

I unfold the dark-red leather-bound guestbook. In six languages, it explains what the hotel can do for the celebrated and thrice-welcomed guest. The lack of breakfast on the night train leaves me hungry, prompting me to peruse the room service menu, which, while not particularly extensive, primarily features gourmet dishes. I ignore the caviar and truffle pasta, as well as the oysters, and call for a roast beef sandwich with parmesan shavings and a pot of coffee. Yes, a whole liter. And why not add a bottle of San Pelegrino, too? I notice that the management is promoting, in particular, a red wine of the year 1917, undoubtedly unaware that this is *l'anno fra i piu tristi della storia d'Italia.* I'm not quite heartless enough to comment on that on the phone—in French. By the way, I don't need the wine. No alcohol at this time. Coffee, my divine drink.

I begin the process of unpacking, a task I never delegate to servants, despite their excellent performance in hotels such as this one. No one needs to know what baggage I carry with me. No man touches my underwear. Despite the legendary discretion that hotels such as this offer, some gossip tends to spread instantly. My comfortable but relatively conventional and inconspicuous travel clothes come off quickly. I sort out some attire I want to wear next, and in the meantime fill the bath with half the contents of a bottle of soap and hot water. Even in first class, I couldn't avoid the lack of comfort on the train from Rome to Venice, which consumed a significant amount of my time and energy. However, it is not worse than some of the railway services in the United Kingdom. I merely compare without judging further. Ten years after the war, we, the victors, are still doing worse in many respects than our former enemies.

Too late, I remember that I opened the window and didn't close the curtains. In the buildings across the canal, however, the windows are dark, but it is not impossible that an attentive peeping tom watches the slightest of my movements and now admires my anatomy—almost completely undressed. Demonstratively, I step towards the window and roughly pull the curtain closed. What I don't know doesn't bother me, and I have never been ashamed of my physique—but still . . .

The bath gives me ample time to consider my situation. There is the letter in my leather briefcase, which I always carry with me. It arrived at my flat in Park Lane two weeks ago, and the concierge treated it with great care. The envelope did not mention the name or address of the sender, which is remarkable in these times. Inside was a single sheet of thick cream-colored paper, of a sort you can only buy in the more expensive shops on Piccadilly. The author used a fountain pen and appeared to have been trained in almost classical calligraphy. His English was absolutely perfect, even a bit posh. I assumed he had a decent education and was a member of the better classes. I would recognize one of them at once, certainly in their handwriting.

The letter informed me I would be very interested in the object the writer wanted to sell me. That in itself upset me. A seller, perhaps of insurance or of real estate in the Bahamas, or of Jewish diamonds looted during the war that would never see their rightful owner again but which I could buy for a bargain price. I would have stopped reading at once, were it not that something about the language intrigued me.

So I read on. The author assured me that he was not a charlatan, that he was not out to separate me from a significant sum of money in any blatantly unethical manner, and that he wanted to sell me an authentically important item. The object held significant historical value, yet it also had the potential to discredit a number of individuals. These people, he specified, belonged to one of our former enemies but should also be considered enemies of humanity. That's why he didn't hesitate to sell this item to me. He made me understand that I was, given my standing in society, the most suitable buyer.

The story is becoming stranger and stranger—such were my thoughts at the time.

I could, the letter continued, be certain that the object had considerable value to humanity. However, the transaction he had in mind required the utmost discretion. He asked me not to discuss this with anyone. That alone suggested intrigue, and enemies, and danger. And it was as if the letter writer knew me well—or at least well enough to know that I have no habit of avoiding intrigue, enemies, and danger. On the contrary, I confront them with a willingness worthy of a better cause.

He hadn't yet disclosed the alluring aspects of his proposal, which he needed to postpone for the time being. We would meet on a certain day in Venice, in a specific coffee house, and at a precise time. That day is tomorrow, and that's why I'm here now.

I cannot—or dare not—explain why I am responding to this letter. A world of possible scenario's presents itself. A charlatan wants to kidnap me and then demand a ransom from my husband's family, who will under no circumstances pay. But someone who would like to kidnap me could do so with much less effort and much less intrigue in London itself. Why must I travel all the way to Venice? Is the potential kidnapper too lazy to go to London, or are his funds insufficient for the trip?

No, that's absurd. I can't imagine what intrigue lies behind this scenario, except that the letter writer certainly has something to sell me. All this gives me a kind of alibi, or a pretext, to leave dusty, stuffy London, if only for a week or so, and visit this city. My parents once stayed here—more than once, in fact—and they later recalled only the good times. In a different era and decade, at the turn of the century and before that other war, the world and future had no limits.

Now that I'm here, I want to savor some of the local culture. The present riddle obviously piques my interest, but I expect it to reveal itself as utterly banal history. I arrived early enough to experience the upcoming *Festa Della Madonna Della Salute*, which always brings a considerable crowd to *La Serenissima*, even so late in the year. Residents of this city are so serene and self-confident that they never miss a chance to party, taking both Christian and pagan opportunities to hide behind masks and vanity. The city is a cliché, but it bears this fate with smooth grace and civilized perseverance.

My watch tells me it's almost time for lunch. "Per questo pasto consiglio un vino rosso," says the waiter in the small restaurant in the alley behind the hotel, and so I follow his advice. At the end of the meal—vongole, pasta—I ask him: "Un cappuccino e una pasta alla crema, per favore." After all, it is not such a complex language, at least not if you have a decent notion of French. I can read an Italian newspaper. Not that the news interests me. Who wants to get involved in Italian politics, and the unpleasant but deep-seated hatred between the communists and the remnants of the semi-fascist middle class? This is the same class that continues to hold the Vatican in high regard, despite its alignment with the fascist rulers. The apostle Peter came to establish his church in the poorest country in western Europe, and in the least religiously inclined. He should have known better, even in his days.

At another table sits a couple; he seriously tanned, she a milky white child. They hardly eat anything, only drink water, and their conversation is equally austere. Every now and then, he or she glances at me, maybe out of curiosity, on account of my clothes, my delicate skin, and my obviously non-Italian origins. Everything about me screams I am a tourist. So they keep an eye on me. Their interest in me is both suspicious and unwelcome. However, I ignore them, not even with as much as a glance. I eat, drink my wine, read the newspaper, carefully sip the cappuccino, savor the pastries, and read some more in the newspaper, although the latter activity is just a pretext to hang around for a while longer. Finally, I pay the waiter, add a generous *pourboire*, get up, and leave the establishment. A little further on, I look in a window. I no longer spot the couple. They don't shadow me. I'm paranoid, but in this city and in this age of spies and nuclear secrets and cold war, every citizen has a right to be paranoid.

3

I avoid introspection. That's what the war taught me. Worrying too much about what's going on inside your head distracts you from what's really important, such as surviving. Survival is the only thing you ought to concentrate on during a war. In 1944, Italy was not so much a battlefield; it was a ruin, where people nevertheless tried to survive. I've heard that the various warring parties literally razed many villages to the ground. As of today, most of them remain in ruins. They may never rise again. The British and Americans believed their planes and artillery would do an excellent job of bombarding the Germans (and their less numerous Italian allies). Afterwards, however, the ruins turned out to be excellent hiding places for snipers and machine gun posts, for infantrymen equipped with Pfantzerfausts, and for fanatical SS troops. Italy became one of the most brutal theaters of the war, second only to Russia.

Ten years later, tourists avoid these places. There is nothing to see; no one lives there anymore. Nature overgrows roads and buildings. The major art cities, however, have been spared. Humanity has always shown more respect for art and culture than for the lives of its individual members. People slaughtered or gassed intellectuals, yet the Renaissance's legacy endured.

Now that I have arrived here, I am pleased enough about this development. Venice, however, is not a bustling city, but is rather subdued, thoughtful, cautious, and reserved. It offers peace of mind, but at the same time it doesn't, because there is too much to see. There are an excessive number of churches, museums, and crumbling, semi-destitute palazzos, all accessible to the public. As a tourist, I would spend a full week here. But I'm not here to be a tourist.

I read the letter once again. Which is useless because I know every word by heart. I notice the carefully constructed sentences that reveal a decent education. This is not a letter from an opportunistic tout. The use of words is too precise; the approach is deliberately seductive but not too intrusive. Whoever wrote this letter knows that I may be willing to exchange certain funds for a remarkable object and be convinced of its authenticity. Whoever wrote this letter knows me. Perhaps they don't know me personally, but they know me well enough to persuade me to visit Venice.

Here I am.

I glance at my watch. It is half past seven. I had no more than a short walk in this city. However, I'm not going to spend the whole evening in my room. I'm not going to hang out in the hotel bar, where undoubtedly expensive escorts will be stalking wealthy foreign businessmen. I once played that role myself, before the war. I was young then, foolish, and I needed money. So I invested in two dresses and some luxurious underwear, had my hair fixed, and headed to the most expensive hotel I could find: the Ritz, on Piccadilly. That was the year 1938, when it was already clear that Germany no longer wanted peace but intended to conquer a good part of Europe. Most people, however, chose to ignore the danger the Nazis posed.

Back then you could still get into the Ritz easily enough after handing the doorman some money—quite a bit of money in my case, but I saw it as a matter of investment. I needed an income after my family withdrew my allowance, while I fully intended to continue living and studying in central London. What else can a girl do under those circumstances? I had no immediate intention of selling my body, at most renting it out to the highest bidder. And what a body it was, if I say so myself! I had completed ten years of ballet, not professionally but seriously enough to develop a slim and muscular figure that adequately compensated for my small breasts and narrow hips. There are men who have no need for a voluptuous woman in bed. So that's what I offered. My dress provided a clear indication of my body type.

But I usually avoid this kind of introspection. I don't want to think about those difficult years anymore. A bit later, I secured a position as a reporter at a major newspaper. Shortly after, I became one of the few female journalists in North Africa, a situation that baffled the army leadership. As a woman with a press card and a letter from the ministry of war, I was granted the authority to accompany the troops under all circumstances. Even then, my body served its purpose perfectly, as few journalists received such a letter and permission.

Afterwards, however, I had ample opportunity to regret my decision to write about the war on the ground. Of course, one develops a thick skin around dirty, exhausted frontline troops. And after seeing a few mutilated corpses (or what remained of them), habituation sets in.

Several men and women notice me as I leave the hotel, likely due to the tight black clothes I wear. Perhaps my attire reminds them of their own fascist past. This black ideology remains stubbornly intertwined with our society, and more so in this country. The petite bourgeoisie is no less averse to Jews and foreigners today than it was twenty years ago. Defeat does not register in people's minds as long as they can continue to hate. Even today, Britain has its share of racial hatred as well.

I walk away from the canal, through the Calle Traghetto Vecchio, where in some places the laundry hangs to dry on the facades, and the sharp voices of housewives can be heard calling their offspring to order. Or their husband. I was spared a progeny. Providence has intervened neatly, albeit unsolicited. Children would only complicate my situation. Mother, me? It's definitely not the role I had in mind. What do you do with kids? They cling to you, and then they leave. I was undoubtedly that kind of child, too. I betrayed my family and paid a price for it, but in the end, my life is only richer for it. In experiences, and also financially.

Further on, I walk through Calle Secheria, which opens up to a small square where the street intersects with the Corte Canal. The Osteria Della Rivetta restaurant is on the right. No woman will dine here alone, except me, and I will get a table because I am a foreigner and because even the most half-blind Italian patron sees I have money. The restaurant is deserted, save for an elderly couple. On the small heated terrace, with only four tables, a man in his fifties brings me cutlery and a neat white napkin, all without a moment's hesitation. Oh yes, Venice and glamour! Gloria Swanson and her daughter recently visited Venice for the film festival, demonstrating their familiarity with opulence.

Night has now fallen. The old-fashioned and, in my opinion, downright dangerous gas lighting has only been replaced by electric light in a few places, and wine bottles with a candle are placed on the tables, adding to the fire risk. Anything for romance, right? I order my second hot meal of the day and a bottle of red wine, and at once a couple of younger guests, foreigners, sit down at one of the other tables, no doubt reassured by my lonely presence. He appears to be cosmopol-itan, dressed in a gray autumn suit, a starched white shirt, and a black tie, while she is dressed in Chanel or something similar. Both of them seem out of place here, as osterias are not typically frequented by wealthy individuals. That is, except by me.

I ordered antipasto and meat, and I'm eating quietly because I have plenty of time, at least for now. The wine is a local variety from a sunny hill here in the Veneto, and it tastes excellent. The couple clearly does not speak Italian and makes do by pointing at the menu. As everywhere, passersby stare at us: tourists won't be common in this or any other Italian city for another decade. We are now exotic animals, misguided travelers in anti-time. I toast a passing older lady, and I can't help but smile.

4

I ignore my dreams with a tenacity worthy of a better cause. Only love sustains us, and love survives only in the future. Dreams, on the other hand, merely imitate the past. They proliferate in the world that is gone forever. With our awakening, they disappear. What existed in the past can no longer hurt me.

There are, however, people who have persevered through the years and continue to pester me today. My almost ex-husband. His family. My family. Those are the survivors. The corpses, on the other hand, don't bother me. They are scattered across the battlefield of my past. They don't turn against me. People only pay the price of the past when others hunt them down. When their past actions are too grotesque to forget or forgive, they pay a price. The Nuremberg trials are an example of this principle. These were necessary to appease Europe's conscience. We had to restore the moral order and initiate the psychological healing process.

The victorious political order desperately needed these processes because, years earlier, it had failed to prevent fascism's rise. This order wished to forget its mistakes as soon as possible. For millions of victims, however, the trials came too late. While we haven't found and convicted all Nazis yet, Nuremberg was a significant beginning. Humanity is unforgiving and vengeful, rightly so. We cannot eradicate abstract evil, but we can weed out its concrete counterpart. But the political will needs to be present. Under current conditions, I doubt this is the case.

The morning is gray but atmospheric. I expect nothing more from Venice than to wrap itself in a misty cloak. The city should live up to its enigmatic reputation. It endured the global crisis, just as the republic it once represented endured various disasters for centuries. I wonder if Catholicism, which has plagued Europe for ages with the stench of musty churches, the fumes of incense, and the horror of unwashed chasubles, still burdens this city. The tolerant heart of the Church of England, hardly a religion but rather an esoteric community that believes in the good of man and admits to a lukewarm relationship with a God never found outside sacred buildings and hallowed grounds, shaped my upbringing. Catholics, on the other hand, belong to a sect with the political urge for world dominance engraved in its corrupt soul. The ruling elite still uses it to oppress their own as well as foreign peoples via this religion. Without her, Venice would not have even existed, and probably not today's Europe either.

The hotel's breakfast room overlooks the canal. On the other side, in front of the railway terminal, the vaporetto dock is busy, crowded even. Here too, commuters are on their way to their jobs, just like they do in London. Almost all are men, in dark overcoats, hats, and even some scarves. The mundane is a boring necessity, especially for those who survived the war.

I spend several unnecessary hours in the alleys and near the canals, the sight of which disappoints me. During previous visits I discovered a miniature city, unreal, too small and cramped, like a decor for some abstract event. It lacks the grandeur of other Italian Renaissance cities. The typical Venetian is also too busy for this narrow city. He—and she—prefers Baroque and lengthy sentences to describe any banal situations (or so I was told by Italian friends from Rome), and does not shy away from the occasional use of Arabic, or the languages of the Maghreb. Not without reason, this city was the main port of the civilized world for centuries—when civilization had not yet reached the North of Europe in all its glory. In those days, the Doges were more powerful than the Pope.

Meanwhile, the hour of the ominous encounter has arrived. I confess to being both worried and nervous, feeling unnecessary and useless. The coffee house is not far from the hotel and not far from where I had dinner last night, on the Calle de la Laca. From the outside, the establishment appears banal, typical, and quite expensive. The facade is in poor condition, as with all buildings in this country. The lack of funds for renovations and maintenance is a result of excessively stringent building regulations and a shortage of skilled artisans. Someone who shouldn't be allowed near brushes has repeatedly painted over the old restaurant sign.

Inside, an imposing counter and a mirrored wall with bottles of spirits take up the entire back, and the establishment is more spacious than I expected. I estimate about thirty tables, half of which are occupied. A diverse crowd, including some foreigners. Amidst the cackle of voices, no one notices me. That's how I prefer it. I should have worn a pantsuit in the latest Parisian fashion instead of my black and leather. No problem, there's will yet be enough time to be eccentric. Immediately, I retrieve a pack of Gauloises from my handbag and ignite one using a Zippo, which I inherited from an American soldier who died near Monte Cassino. It bears his name engraved on its bottom.

I take a deep drag on the cigarette. I prefer this brutal French tobacco, superior to the effeminate rubbish my countrymen smoke. A waiter approaches reluctantly, and I order a Crodino and a plate of *stuzzichini salati*, even though I'm not hungry. Everything is delivered quickly. I sip my drink, consume my snack, and survey my surroundings. Now that I'm a static target, glances are being cast at me. Blonde, pale, foreign. Some young men consider their chances with me. I return their gaze coolly, and affirm their odds are visibly dim. I know I'm too early—ten or fifteen minutes—but that's how I approach the problem strategically. I am so often, pathologically even, too early.

Either the man recognizes me somehow, or he has no difficulty picking me out in this collection of guests because he immediately sits down at my table. "Signora Barth," he says. "My name is Edvardo, and I am the person who wrote you a letter."

He is (I assume) in his mid-forties, already balding, thin, quite tall, vaguely Mediterranean, and his English is softened by a pleasant accent that women love to hear in Italian men. Not me. I don't care about their accent. I don't care for Italian men either. During my war, I encountered numerous Italian men, often in less than ideal circumstances. I'm not impressed by him.

Especially since he is not Italian. His skin and hair tell a story of southern provenance, but he could hail from anywhere in the south of Europe. His accent, when he addresses the waiter, is not authentic; even I can hear that. He has been in this country for a long time and speaks the language fluently, but he was not born here. He speaks too precisely, too correctly. Like me, he is a foreigner.

"You have something for me," I say, getting to the point straight away. This is a commercial transaction, not a marriage proposal. "You expect me to come all the way to Venice to look at what you're offering." That's not true: I would have fled England anyway, even if only for a few weeks, and Venice didn't seem like a disastrous choice. Of course he doesn't need to know that.

He has requested a coffee from the waiter, patiently awaits its arrival, and then proceeds to open the brown leather briefcase he carries. A briefcase, as if he were a bank clerk or a notary. There is a cardboard envelope inside, packed tightly with documents. He takes it out of the bag. I immediately noticed that the documents have a history and have passed through many hands. He runs his fingers over the sheets, so I can see what they are. A collection of handwritten texts. Some of the sheets use letterhead. I recognize that letterhead.

"And what exactly . . ." I ask. If these are merely documents and reports, I'm not inclined to scrutinize them in detail.

"It's something special," he says. "It's not just *anything.*" He pushes the folder with the documents back into his bag. "If you want to inspect them in more detail, then certainly not here. People might recognize . . ." The letterhead—that's what he means. Yes, everyone would recognize it at once.

He drinks his coffee. No sugar, just black. I have another bite. I drink a sip of Crodino.

"Don't expect me to follow you to some shady and suspect place," I warn him.

"I understand your concern, madam. There's no need for that. I have your best interests at heart, believe me. I propose a public library not far from here, where we can go without anyone noticing. There you can view these documents discreetly."

"Then why didn't we meet there in the first place?"

He glances at me but doesn't answer. He doesn't really excel at this game and is clearly not a conspirator, a spy, or a secret agent. I am simply being pursued by an individual who desires to involve me in his game, which I am unwilling to do.

"What did I just see?" I inquire.

"Did you recognize the letterhead?"

"I did," I say.

"Then you know where these documents come from."

Nazi-Germany. That's where those documents come from. Researchers continue to unearth previously unknown German documents every week or so, a decade after the final victory. Sometimes, people have kept these documents hidden for a long time and now want to cash in on them. There are plenty of potential buyers for stuff like this. Historians, private collectors, a few secret services, and probably some very shady characters. They want to get their hands on everything that was ever put on paper in Nazi Germany. I've read about entire warehouses filled with documents. There will never be enough historians to study all of them. On account the importance of understanding the origins and history of Evil, it might be beneficial to have as much knowledge as possible.

"I know what you're thinking," he says.

"What am I thinking?"

"Even more papers without historical interest."

"I'm not a specialist," I say. "Why do you think I would be interested at all?"

"It's a diary," he says.

"It is?"

"And not just from anyone," he continues. He narrows his eyes. "No, not Hitler's diaries. That would really be . . ." He coughs nervously.

"Who then?"

He leans forward. The name he is about to pronounce is damning, or incriminating. The name he is going to pronounce may not be spoken aloud in public. There is a curse on it. "It's Alfred Rosenberg's diary," he says.

Then he sits up again and waits for my reaction. I was at the front. Ask me which hamlets were destroyed, where the corpses were piled up, and where a terrible fate awaited children and women. I provide a complete list.

The names of the men behind these horrors, none of whom I ever met? Yes, they are all equally etched in my memory. I read them in newspapers, magazines, and books. I remembered them all.

Like Rosenberg's.

He gets up. "Follow me," he says.

5

The library is situated in one of those inscrutable, constantly musty palazzos to which Venice seems to have exclusive rights. Not all of them are built on stilts in the water, but they all suffer from rising dampness. We're actually in a sea lagoon. Venice resembles a poorly maintained vessel, anchored against its will at a distance from any decent port, and unable to regain its buoyancy. It is a fatal, dramatic city, a victim of its own reputation and history.

The color of the facade may once have been red, or perhaps brown, or something in between, but now it looks as if a capricious and undisciplined child has smeared various shades of dirty orange paint over the plasterwork. The windows need to be cleaned of cobwebs and dust. The gate is wide open, and the interior is cool, dry, dusty. I'm not betting money on the longevity of paper in this city, but the books seem to have found a relatively safe haven.

Edvardo, who still has no surname, precedes me. He apparently comes here more often. We ascend a wide stone staircase on the right, then pass an empty room with bookcases (we are in a library, after all). Next, we enter a smaller room where no one is visible. He sits down at a table near a window that looks out onto a courtyard and the rear of other buildings. The table and chairs have been eaten by woodworms. He deposits the briefcase on the table and slides out the cardboard folder, opens it, and shows me the documents.

A gray cloth-bound book, about two hundred pages. Next, a pile of unbound pages, brimming with notes on both sides, each bearing a date. The sheets are of various formats, as if the writer wrote down his thoughts on everything within reach. Most of them display the letterhead of a ministry, department, or whatever. Eagles and swastikas decorate everything, leaving no doubt about their origin. I can't read German, so I can't check what the author assigned to the paper.

"In the spring of 1945," Edvardo begins, "American soldiers visiting Schloss Banz, in Bavaria, discovered a collection of documents belonging to a dubious aristocrat, Kurt von Behr, who had spent part of the war in Paris. He'd hidden important documents in his basement, he told the soldiers. He then pompously committed suicide. Alfred Rosenberg, the Nazi Party's chief ideologue and close friend of Adolf Hitler, authored those documents, which included his private diary. In it, he described the course of events at the highest level of the NSDAP, starting in 1934, the year after Hitler's takeover. He detailed the responsibilities of many high-ranking Nazis as well as his own. Although moral objections did not exactly plague him during his own trial, this all turned out to be very distressing reading."

"He wasn't the only one who left a diary, wasn't he?"

"No, the same was true for Goebbels and Hans Frank, the governor of occupied Poland. However, Rosenberg was not of the same caliber as other Nazis. He was an intellectual, although not of the highest order. For years, he exerted significant influence on Hitler and, consequently, on Nazi Germany's politics. He organized the major theft of art treasures in the occupied territories, using the excuse that their owners had abandoned them, no one claimed them anymore, and Germany had taken them into safe custody for the benefit of all humanity."

"A lot of transparent lies," I respond. "The rightful owners met their demise in concentration camps."

"Indeed, but this was the defense Rosenberg presented during his trial in Nuremberg. Anyway, he headed the occupation authorities in the Baltic states, Belarus, and Ukraine, where he helped organize the genocide of Jews. He also previously laid out the ideological and—we may say with some poetic license—philosophical basis for those atrocities when he published *Der Mythus des 20. Jahrhunderts*, an inaccessible and failed philosophical book that nevertheless achieved almost as large a circulation as *Mein Kampf* and which was required reading for all Nazi officials."

"And he was convicted in Nuremberg?"

"He was hanged on October 16, 1946. During that trial, the prosecutor, Robert Kempner, an American of German origin who himself narrowly escaped the Nazis, used the diary as one of the incriminating documents. It was supposed to be kept in the United States after the trial but was lost. Nobody knows what happened to it."

"And now you have it here."

"Indeed."

"And it still is of historical importance."

"There is more than historical importance," he continues. "If it was just that, I would sell it to the American Holocaust Museum. They definitely would want it. Or to a wealthy collector. But now . . . Your past makes you the best candidate to make this document public."

"Wealthy collectors of Nazi memorabilia are difficult to find, I suppose. Not many people want to get involved with that part of German history anymore."

"More than you assume, Signora Barth. More than you assume. There are plenty of people who look back with misplaced nostalgia at the Germany of a decade or two before the war. The right people were in power, if you asked large parts of the middle class and the wealthy at the time. The mob no longer ruled the streets, life and limb were safe, inflation was under control, the communists were in camps, as well as those terrible Jews."

"But there was violence and . . ."

"It is difficult for us to imagine this now, signora, but for the average German, who did not suffer from persecution himself, the rise of the NSDAP and Hitler was a blessing. Germany was humiliated in 1918; then there was civil war, blind violence, everyone was hungry, enormous poverty. People needed security and a future, even if it meant dealing with the black uniforms and the pathological speeches. Populism is a powerful force in politics, and the masses only think with their stomachs and their wallets, not with their common sense. And they certainly don't show moral or ethical considerations. However, that kind of nostalgia is not without danger, because fascism, to which these people look back so helplessly, will resurface time and time again, even in Western democracies. Don't underestimate the persistence of hatred!"

"Why me? Why are you approaching me?"

"Ah," he says. "First of all, you have money. Second, you've been there. The war, I mean. You have personally experienced the effects of extreme and blind hatred. You can be my go-between by being beyond doubt about your motives. I don't expect you to acquire the diary for yourself. You buy it for a fair price, and then you make sure it falls into the right hands, of individuals capable of averting a fresh outbreak of the dark menace. Too many fascists are still at large. You're in a better position than I am to negotiate with . . . well, with anyone."

"I don't understand your problem. Why do you need an intermediary?"

His smile is a forced grimace, an attempt to suppress shame. "I am far from an impeccable citizen, Signora Barth. My past would make this manuscript suspicious. I also don't want to reveal how I obtained this diary. You, on the other hand, buy it from an anonymous source; you belong to the upper British class, and after your career as a war correspondent no one will suspect you of right-wing sympathies."

It's absurd. That's what I tell him. A collector or institution can easily verify the authenticity of these documents. They are more of historical interest than ideological. Why wouldn't he sell them himself? His past? Why does that matter?

He takes a deep breath. "I was a member of the Waffen-SS," he says. "Do you require any further explanation? I was involved in some of the war's darkest episodes, details of which I do not wish to share with you, nor with others. I don't want people looking into my past. I have done things that, in this new world, must remain hidden forever. Signora, I was more than just a follower. Naivety is my only excuse, but no one will take that into account. At the time, I was proud of what I did for my country and the party. I was proud of my black uniform. Today I think differently, but I have no intention of publicly confessing my regret or taking responsibility for my actions. So that's my problem."

Waffen-SS. I can envision scenarios involving Poland, Russia, camps, prisoners of war, genocide, the Holocaust, and mass killings of civilians. The list of crimes against humanity is very extensive. Many stories have surfaced over the past decade. He doesn't have my sympathy. I have seen, with my own eyes, what fanatical Nazi supporters did in the occupied territories and even in their own country. As for me . . .

But I'm distancing myself. From him, from the proposal. From the diary.

The diary—that's what this is about. Until now, it only served as evidence to convict Rosenberg and other Nazi leaders. Now it can point at people who are still in power. As such, it deserves to be made public. The horror at the hands of a man like Edvardo is one thing. He was a tool for men far more powerful than himself. One of those men wrote this diary.

But then, I don't want to think about getting involved in this. I would like to pass on that honor. History and especially historiography can do without me. Even a footnote is too much honor.

"On the other hand, there are people," I say, "who would rather see this disappear. Even today."

"That's a correct conclusion," he says. "In their opinion, these notes should not even exist."

"And so the possession of this diary is . . ."

". . . dangerous. Indeed. For me. And for you as well. But no one will know you have it."

The situation is unreal. His motives are unconvincing. I have other things on my mind at this particular moment.

The only thing that can convince me is my experience during the war. Behind stories, legends, and myths, lies a truth. The man who wrote this diary was a psychopath, a monster. I read about his trial, as well as that of the other monsters. Each of them laid the blame for the horror, for the genocide, elsewhere, claiming to know nothing, claiming never to have actually been involved, and certainly never admitting to having been responsible for the murder of millions of people. They had—in their opinion—merely been civil servants, cogs in a complex machine, sometimes important cogs, but never really in control of that machine. That had been Hitler. And Goebbels.

And others who were already deceased before the Allies could capture them.

This diary proves otherwise. It proves all of these cogs had been responsible for the working of a totalitarian and murderous state. The prosecutor, Kempner, had briefly lifted the veil during the Nurenberg trials, proving the extent of responsibilities. Afterwards, this document disappeared. I can help make it public again, so that people can discover the true face of evil.

But why me? I have other cats to flog. For a while yet, I will have my hands full with that flogging.

"I'm sorry," I tell him. "I don't think I want to help you. Or can. I don't want to take this risk any more than you do. Besides, I have other things to deal with. My life, for one thing."

He sighs and, with an almost dramatic gesture, shoves the whole package back into his briefcase. He is disappointed, but hides it as best he can. "Nonetheless, I'll leave you some time to think about it," he says. "Although I don't know you personally, you're the only one I can trust. Are you staying in Venice for a while longer?"

"A few days."

"A few days. I hope I can speak to you before you leave. Maybe . . ."

I shake my head. "I don't think you can change my mind," I say.

6

Before I continue with my entertaining story, let me introduce my husband. This is him, Michael Holzman-Smith, with the double surname so beloved by the upper British class. His aristocratic appearance, particularly his straight, sharp nose and strong chin, is equally popular. He fits perfectly in the cenacles of the British upper class and the nobility. One of his close ancestors was a fighter pilot during the previous global conflict, and you can imagine *his* profile adorning many a painting, in uniform or in full flying attire. Military museums and private family collections hold these paintings. They symbolize the power of the British Empire. The now largely *former* British Empire.

Michael distinguished himself as a tank commander in North Africa and afterwards in France, so on at least one occasion I may have nearly crossed his path. Tobruk perhaps, who knows. Much later, after the war, at a charity dinner I attended in other company in London, we started a conversation. By then, I assume, he must have heard of me. Fortunately, the reputation I had after the war was very different from that before it, when I tried to live a discreet but sinful life, preying on the corruptions of others.

At the charity dinner, I found myself in excellent company, specifically the Vice Secretary of the Admiralty. At that time, the

Vice Secretary and I had a professional relationship (he wanted me to write his biography, which never happened). The woman I had been before the war no longer existed, and I assumed he had no idea about my antecedents. Michael, probably intrigued by me (I've never been sure of his real feelings), started chatting me up, in that civilized and charming way of his. One thing led to another, and without much delay, there was a marriage proposal, which I accepted.

Lord Holzman-Smith (who was already a Peer of the Realm and sat in the House of Lords, spending everybody's money but his own) probably didn't care who or what I was, as long as I was (a) presentable, (b) straight-talking, (c) discreet, and finally (d) willing to grant his lordship all the liberties he thought he had a right to claim. Well, I could live with all that, in exchange for the luxury his Lordship was willing to share with me. At the start of our relationship, I was certainly accommodating and willing to accommodate this gentleman generously—and ask for very, very little in return.

It is still strange (in particular from my point of view) that a man like him did not find a more suitable match in his own social circles, and sought refuge with a famous yet rather common (in many senses of the word) journalist and former war correspondent. I always suspected he wanted to upset his family, although no one has spoken to me about this in so many words. However, it seems to me to be the only rational explanation for his decision to marry me, even now.

Suddenly, I found myself fully prepared for life, leveraging my experience to seamlessly integrate with his environment. The latter, in particular, was helpful to me. I managed to blend in very well with my surroundings and become one of the upper class, although I was barely accepted by them.

Michael wasn't my first man (at least not in the possessive, sexual sense), and he wasn't my first love (because I didn't really love him). Let that much be clear.

Anyway, from that moment on, I had my life fully in order. At most, I had to avoid the Ritz hotel, as well as other places where I could be recognized, as well as men who had used my services more than a decade earlier, even though they almost certainly wouldn't recognize me. Three weeks into our wedding (a quick affair in a remote Scottish village, with twenty guests in a droughty castle, and two half-hearted attempts at sex on his part), Michael took me to a reception at that same famous Ritz, but there happened to be no one with whom I had previously shared a couch or a bed.

However, I knew very quickly that my new husband had not exactly married me for my skills in bed, my attractive body, or my other physical charms. We made out a few times more, with less than mixed success, and from then on he avoided me. I realized I had married a man who was not interested in women but didn't want to stand out socially.

Noblesse oblige, or something.

I would have been willing to show a certain largesse in the face of this neglect. After all, I wasn't exactly an angel, even if he didn't know my pre-war past. But I soon noticed that he was not really averse to sex, although solely with his own gender.

Things started to occur to me. He paid close attention to younger men, both in public and private settings; he refrained from explaining his extended absences, and he avoided opening certain letters in my presence. A young servant who left his room late at night then disappeared from duty without any explanation from Michael's side. No one told me anything, mainly because I had no girlfriends and none of his family hung out with me much. A wall of silence surrounded me.

Then I found him in bed with a young man, *en flagrant délit*.

7

A sudden arising fog accompanies my quite appropriate dramatic thoughts. Yet here, in a city where it appears normal for buildings to float one meter above the ground, fog is an acceptable part of daily life. You can always count on atmospheric particularities when your thoughts threaten to descend into the underworld, as mine do. At the hotel desk, they assure me that it will not rain today and that I do not need an umbrella. Still, I ought to be careful, they warn me, because the fog not only limits visibility but is also responsible for slippery stairs and tiles. So watch out, Signora!

I will do that. I will watch out. Evil intentions, but also unfaithful lovers, may hide in the mist, because this is Venice, where intrigue and death and dramatic love stories are etched into every wall, and not a letter is written without spreading a lie. The canals, with their greasy bollards and anachronistic gondolas, spread a stale, earthy smell that reminds me of the ground freshly churned up by mortar shells elsewhere in Italy, always a prelude to the stench of decomposing carcasses of people and animals.

The implications of the bargain are now clear to me: I am offered a dubious Nazi document, out of the guilty hands of someone who once belonged to the camp of my enemies. Perhaps such is still the case. Is it possible to cure a faithful follower, indoctrinated and imbued with an evil ideology, and transform them into a normal human being? This is more than just a theoretical philosophical question, and my life might depend on the answer.

But what is a normal person? Most of those accused at Nuremberg (all seated defiantly or apparently indifferently on their benches) appeared normal, considered themselves normal, professed a normal lifestyle (home, garden, children) and merely followed orders or instructions. For them, at least according to their claims, Evil was always festering elsewhere: in the minds, beliefs and imaginations of other people, in other homes and in other ministries, in other geographical places, while extermination camps and execution grounds and ovens existed out there, in a world beyond their responsibility.

Fighting such aberrant beliefs is still surprisingly complex, even today. A decade after the war, the profound convictions of those on the evil side of history have not changed. On the contrary. Today, the average Italian, German, or even British citizen will not be hospitable to those who come from foreign countries, have a different skin color, or practice a different religion. They will hate those who find refuge in their country and who threaten their religious beliefs and their jobs. Human nature does not change, not even after all the cruelty that has come to light in the previous decade.

Should I have accepted the stack of manuscripts at face value, in exchange for a check from Lloyds Bank? Wouldn't my banker send me a telegram, after a few days, to inquire whether I really intended to hand over such a significant sum to a potentially suspicious third party? Is there a mechanism in place to safeguard me against my insanity and the deceit of others?

But none of this happened. Edvardo and I parted ways, without promises. He the man with the false Italian name and the false Italian appearance, I the poor excuse for his moral salvation. Wasn't that precisely what he sought? Moral salvation? Would he have handed over the manuscript to me without any form of payment if I had freed him of his demons? I strongly suspect so. But not right away. Not without asking for money first.

Indeed, the stairs appear slippery, as do some of the tiles on sidewalks and alleys. I move cautiously. A fine mist is descending, not rain. Men who pass me take shelter under umbrellas, often with a woman on their arm. Someone has taken in the laundry and is currently ironing it. Coffee is made in those typical dented espresso cookers, while in the kitchen children play with wooden blocks and rag dolls. I don't know how an average household functions, but I can easily imagine scenes like that.

I am now wearing my black leather trousers, gray calfskin boots, white blouse and my wool-lined aviator jacket, and I may be mistaken by some of the passersby for a somewhat exaggeratedly slim young man, until they notice the shape of my hips and my bosom. No, not my bosom. The jacket conceals what little progress I've made in that area. So the hips have to do it, although they are not exactly Rubensian either. They contrast poorly with the voluptuous display of flesh in Renaissance nudes, which make their joyful appearance in local museums. I will pay them a visit the next few days, those naked ladies, as I am here and have nothing more demanding to do.

Nothing to do? The world intervenes somewhat harshly at my return to the hotel, when the receptionist—another young man—discreetly beckons me closer. He has received a telephone message for me, and I can call a number back in my room. Signora. Thank you. It's a British number. I call and get my lawyer on the line. Edward Ellison Morse, Esq., who defends my private interests against the barbarian legions of my in-laws, and as such he guarantees my private allotment of order and civilization. His interventions and their outcome involve a lot of money, potentially anyway. As long as I receive adequate compensation for the pain and humiliation, my hopefully soon-to-be former husband may continue to share the bed with other men at his own discretion. And there are still some more arguments that I can and will put forward to further my case, all under the expert guidance of Master Morse, who is a thorough and, above all, experienced specialist in divorce cases and their associated legal implications. He has already drawn up numerous documents, all in perfect but baffling legalese, providing the necessary arguments in my favor.

"However, a problem has recently and unexpectedly emerged," he says testily. And even despite the poor connection between my homeland and Venice, his voice sounds concerned. Well, not so much concerned as annoyed. "His attorney argues that the testimony against your husband we provided is biased and that there is no actual tangible evidence of his infidelity and his . . ."

"He fucked that guy in the . . ."

"Probably," says Morse, as always testifying to the extremely civilized personality that he displays in court and with which he stands his ground when faced with the cretinous (his term) mob on the other side of the barrier—meaning the lawyers of the opposing party. Undoubtedly, he also refers to the common people in the public gallery. "He is probably guilty of those reprehensible acts, of fornication and buggery, of infidelity and disloyalty, and so on. There is a wealth of circumstantial evidence, as well as testimonies. But it depends on which judge we face, Mrs. Barth. Or which jury. Everything depends on that."

I imagine him in his office on Chancery Lane, surrounded (maybe even besieged) by Victorian furniture, Edwardian hunting pictures, and never-consulted (and therefore excessively dusty) tomes, in that office with the dark brown wooden paneling. His surroundings couldn't be more classic and civil, with his assistants and junior solicitors in the larger office next to his, all of them young men who are at his every beck and call, who are prepared to work long hours to present the correct and most applicable legal arguments for any of his pending cases. They excel in locating evidence, questioning witnesses, and crafting documents. I wonder if his army also does other things—things at a further distance from what is legally allowed, such as pressuring witnesses, fabricating false testimonies, and other such activities that a solid law firm like his should keep far away from. I never inquired and don't plan to.

In his possession, he has a signed statement from my husband's love interest. What more does he want? What more does he need? Divine intervention?

"The respected opposing party's lawyer will argue that the incriminating testimony was obtained under pressure, that it does not entirely correspond to reality, that the witness was bribed, and what not. Plenty of arguments, actually. And perhaps some of those arguments are not far from the truth. The judge then wants to see the prosecution witness appear on the stand, but he does not show up because he does not want adverse publicity and shame. Therefore, the matter remains unresolved. Without that testimony, we don't actually have much of a case."

"We have to catch him," I implore, "red-handed, as they say. We, and not just me. You. The police. You undoubtedly are acquainted with some police officers who are eager enough to catch someone like my husband red-handed, in bed?"

"Evidently," he says measuredly.

"What do you mean?" He doesn't seem fully convinced by my arguments.

"Something like that can be arranged," he agrees. Not willing to pursue this line of reasoning, not over the phone anyway.

"By which you mean that you are actually going to arrange it. And before you tell me this is going to cost money. Well, it may cost money. Money is—I don't shy away from a cliché—no objection. I'm sure you are well aware of my specific situation."

"We haven't had this conversation, Mrs. Barth," he says matter-of-factly.

Obviously, we haven't had this conversation. I've had so many conversations that did not happen. The majority of these occurred during my heyday in London, shortly before the war. My years of deception and illusions. So many men I haven't seen, whom I haven't spoken to, who haven't shared my bed. But Morse will do what I ask of him, with almost proverbial discretion, and then send me a bill for costs he has not incurred, which I will of course pay.

In the end, however, my husband will stand in the dock facing accusations of dishonorable practices, specifically fornication with a person of the same gender, a crime for which the hypocritical society in the United Kingdom lacks an official name. Oh, yes, yes. *Sodomy*, I believe it is called. Regardless of the term, it carries severe penalties. Michael goes to jail, and I then get a good part of his fortune in the divorce, as well as compensation from his family.

That's the plan.

8

I am exploring the neighborhood, looking for a restaurant that may be suitable for my modest tastes, preferably one that offers local cuisine. It's half past seven, which, in this country, may be too early for dinner, but I don't care what Italians think of me or how they live their lives. I was never impressed by their civil society and customs, and even less by their hedonistic lifestyle. The further south one travels in Europe, the less inclined people are towards hard work and self-improvement. My personal opinion. Although they have to make an effort, under certain circumstances. Generations of farmers and workers have, against their nature, almost literally worked themselves to death. But the middle and upper class? The civil servants, those employed by the government? The people owning a shop or a private business and being their own boss? Not so much.

This country has always been characterized by a general and widespread culture of procrastination and a deep lack of urgency. We northerners find it difficult to comprehend how such a society is expected to function, and it certainly doesn't. Who can really conduct a decent business when lunch takes two to three hours? When agreements keep getting postponed, decisions delayed. When no plan ever reaches a final stage? When a bribe has to change hands for any venture to be concluded?

I have left the aviator jacket in my room and am wearing a dove-gray mid-length coat in the latest Parisian fashion, which doesn't quite match my leather trousers, but who cares? I just have to say this about the Venetians: they invented not only the income tax but also the noble art of statistics, censorship, the lottery (at least in its modern sense), the ghetto, and finally the glass mirror. Some of these inventions testify to their vanity and fickleness. I am especially grateful for the mirror.

Then there is Venice, the city itself. For many centuries, this scheming republic seduced the most diverse artists and conmen, who often left it to die elsewhere. I can't blame these people. The main reason you don't want to die in Venice is that, as a foreigner, you are not eligible for burial inside its jurisdiction. After a while, however, you discover that you can no longer live without Venice either, at least if I must believe the poets and writers who lost their hearts and senses here. And there are quite a lot of them.

An inverted gondola rests on a wider part of the quay, like half of a beached ancestral animal. Two young men scrape its bottom. Dirt, shellfish—everything has to go. This job requires grace and drive, but evidently at a leisurely pace. That gondola isn't going anywhere, and neither is the dirt. Whatever filth accumulates in these streets and canals is here to stay for an infinite time. Venice recycles all of itself; that's how far this city's independence goes. However, according to Byron, the city is the mask of Italy: not what it is but what it pretends to be is paramount to its culture.

The architecture of Venice mainly aims to create space for shadows. Everything that absorbs the natural light here is loved and cherished. Even the most divine finds itself lost in the unavoidable nocturnal darkness, making the struggle for eternity and a full life futile. So much zeal for just a tad of atmosphere. No wonder that both residents and visitors like to wear masks on festive occasions: they know they are being watched from the dark corners and shady folds of the city and therefore need to conceal their identity.

Dusk lasts for several hours now, while I walk through the alleys and along the canals. My hand carelessly caresses mossy stones and crumbling cement. The lagoon will eventually swallow this city, reducing it to ruins long before it sinks. I pass a few trattorias, filled with tourists and locals alike, sitting at haphazardly placed tables. A British newspaper, in a shabby rack at a gloomy tobacconist, announces the end of the dockers' strike in the old country. Algeria is increasingly confronting the French with organized armed resistance. Russia is a universal enemy, except for the European communists, who cannot keep quiet about their ideological brethren's wonderful achievements.

Ultimately, I choose a restaurant without looking at the posted menu. Like everywhere else one is supposed to order the obligatory three dishes. I definitely overindulge in eating in this city. A healthy breakfast tomorrow, I promise myself. No more pasta, either. I must make amends.

At the table, I look at the couples and wonder what their secret is. What is their secret to living together in apparent harmony, what is the secret to a long and happy marriage, what is the secret to meeting the right person in life? The person who suits you, as if he or she is your double. How do some people manage? Some have unraveled this secret, even at a young age; others plan and mold their togetherness until harmony becomes self-evident.

But both phenomena are clearly to be distinguished from each other. I knew older couples who seemed made for each other but who assured me that they had gone through difficult times. Together, they triumphed over these challenges, avoiding excessive compromises, excessive commitment, or self-loss. However, their efforts reveal that their harmony did not come naturally to them. It is the result of a lifelong effort.

After I take my seat, a man enters the restaurant. The establishment is small, with fifteen tables, for two or four people each. Only half of them are occupied, but there are three busy waiters trotting around who create extra work by chaotically clearing the tables or bringing the dishes separately. It's a family business, I assume, and all the distant cousins need to have jobs.

The man who just came in is wearing a dark blue woolen overcoat, a suit of excellent quality, and holds his hat in his hand. He's not Italian; that much is clear. I immediately notice his eyes: cool, hard. He is balding, although he may not yet be forty-five. He must have been in the war, but I suspect not at the front. I easily identify those who were at the front. Even after a decade, they behave differently than this man.

My pasta arrives, steaming. I sip my white wine for a moment. I observe. And I remember. Ten years ago, I found myself in a different part of Italy. Close to the Monastery of Santa Maria Annunziata, just south of the Reno River, a Canadian sergeant was shot in the head while talking to me. Elsewhere, a mine blew up two Italian anti-fascists in British uniform, just ten paces from where I crouched behind a row of sandbags, their blood coloring my hair red. There is much more. Every war has more to offer, yet those who were present tend to remain silent about it, unless they choose to write a novel. I didn't. Not a novel.

During the war, soldiers dig deep foxholes. After the war, they dig deeper, but only in their heads. Deeper and deeper, to hide everything they experienced.

This man, seated at the other table, has visited haunted places, but I'm still not convinced that it was the battlefield. I want to remember him, so I call him The Bald Man. Maybe I'll never see him again after this. He'll travel on to his mysterious destination tonight, and this meeting, such as it is, will have been a coincidence. But I feel like he's here because I am here. I know it almost with certainty because of this one seemingly insignificant detail: of all those present in this restaurant, he is the only one who does not look at me at any time.

After this observation, I take it easy. I eat the fish and the accompanying salad. I order a coffee after dessert, which allows me some more time at the table. I lean back, openly look at the other guests, note the amorous glances of couples, I note how most of the men are immersed in their newspapers, but they will leave soon enough. I note that there are no women dining alone here, and that's why I stand out (that, and my blonde hair, my clothes, and everything about me that screams I'm not Italian). I note The Bald Man is sitting with his left shoulder towards me and has an eye on everything except me.

I settle my bill and leave. I walk quietly down the street (reddish gaslight, almost equally reddish electric light). The area is largely deserted. The perfect opportunity for an opportunistic criminal. The water in the canals is as black as the ink with which Proust and Chateaubriand used to amaze the world. I look casually over my shoulder, but no one seems to follow me. A little further on, the alleys are a bit busier, and after fifteen minutes I reach my hotel. Somewhat relieved, yes, but also intrigued by the man. I wonder about the reason for his interest in me.

No news awaits me at the hotel. No phone calls, no telegram, nothing. It's all a bit disappointing. I could use some excitement. I intend to travel back to London earlier than expected, now that the main reason for my coming here appears to have been a mistake.

9

The alarm clock on the gilded rococo bedside table tells me that it is half past three in the morning, and I should actually be fast asleep. This is a sleep that is often unfairly bestowed upon the innocent. The idea is ridiculous: no one is truly innocent. Each of our actions arises from pure self-interest and therefore harms someone else. People temporarily lose their common sense when they risk their lives for their fellow humans. As such they are, in every respect, atypical. In any other case, they seek fame. Either way, they are not innocent.

This is the same clock that I bought in London before the war and that lay unused in my flat for years afterwards, while I crawled deep in the dust of war zones, where time has a completely different meaning. War conditions, particularly in a combat zone, obliterate any rational understanding of time. Rest periods are endless moments of boredom and anticipation. You know official history is being written elsewhere, and you want to be there, because you are a journalist, a war correspondent, a reporter, and it is therefore your job to preserve for eternity what that same eternity would rather not be reminded of.

But when the grenades fall, the bullets whizz, people around you die, time is compressed into discrete seconds, each filled with pain and fear, and those seconds last forever. Even the relative peace of a pause in combat is terrifying, as you know that the torment will resume immediately. Some can't handle it. I saw soldiers die of fear and disorientation because they left cover at the wrong time, sometimes even on purpose.

It is still deep night here, as indicated by my faithful clock. I want to sleep, but I can't. Is it the wine? Is it the revelation of Edvardo and his proposal rejected by me? Have I acted incorrectly? Should I have acted differently?

Should I have left this city immediately and returned to my private battles in London? Would that have been the better strategy?

These numerous questions also hinder my ability to sleep.

I get up and drink a glass of tap water. I hesitate in front of the window and peer between the curtains. Few lights illuminate the buildings to the side of the ferry terminal, on the quay, and across the street. The entire neighborhood is almost dark and deserted, although I hear voices. Muffled, soft voices, a man and a woman. Maybe a couple standing on their terrace here in the hotel, admiring the city at night. Venice invites romance; such is its trademark today. People don't come here merely for the museums and churches. Lots of people seek the ultimate romantic experience, although few can afford the local hotels. I haven't had to worry about the cost of accommodation or travel in recent years, thanks to Lloyds Bank and my husband's wealth. In a few months, when I am divorced, I will have even fewer financial constraints.

My impending divorce. This problem wakes me up from my usually not very deep sleep at unwanted moments, because despite the expertise of my lawyer and his office, things can still go seriously wrong. We have taken our precautions, and the trial has been well prepared, but certain elements of this process may be beyond our control. We may need to intensify our efforts towards a positive outcome. The idea of having my husband caught committing a criminal act again seems like a beneficial idea. But is it also practically feasible?

The conversation I didn't have with Morse gives me quasi-certainty that he can arrange something along those lines, but such an endeavor comes with certain risks. Risks for all parties involved, for me, for Morse, and for the young man who will serve as a lure. Morse probably has the same young man in mind who has already appeared willing to entrust a statement under oath to paper. Morse pays him, I'm sure. Whatever Morse does, he does not share with me, because I must remain ignorant and must be able to maintain my ignorance in a court of law. The young man, previously plucked from my husband's bed (so to speak, because they weren't actually caught, except by me), continues his role in this drama. He's already been paid; now he just has to continue down the path he has taken, as a credible prosecution witness. And now, Morse wants him back in on the act.

That's the plan. For now, it's just a plan.

I'm trying to remember that young man's name. I'm unsure if I've heard his name mentioned at some point. There's no need, however. Let him remain, as far as I'm concerned, an anonymous and barely visible participant in this drama. I don't need to know his name until I see him on the witness stand and hear it spoken by the court clerk during my husband's trial and when he talks my husband into jail. Then he assumes the role he is expected to play. Afterwards, he may once more vanish from my existence.

The young man is likely to reach a settlement with the court, receive immunity in exchange for a full confession, and at the most face a fine for his homosexual acts. Nevertheless, he's in trouble because he's been picked up by the police. If he doesn't have something valuable to offer, such as my husband's head, he too will be sentenced to ten years in prison. We all know what happens in prison to young men like him.

Am I losing sleep over this? Rather not. The details of this case are being handled by Master Morse and his assistants. I don't need to intervene. I am a victim, although only indirectly. Nevertheless, because of my husband's behavior, I will be able to get my hands on a significant portion of his assets, and that is what ultimately matters. Neglected all these years, subjected to humiliation and exploitation—it has a price, and that price will soon be paid. Some fag can suffer for that. The young man, I mean.

It's quiet outside now. The man and woman on the balcony have probably gone to sleep. I wouldn't mind doing the same. I don't have anything on my agenda tomorrow, but I'll look around the city. If I'm tired of Venice (yes, such is possible, just like you can be tired of London, although you may then be tired of life itself, as Samuel Johnson once claimed), then I'll leave again. Maybe I'll take a train to the French Riviera or have a private driver take me there. November can be quite pleasant on the Riviera. It's where the European Belle Monde settles to spend the winter. I will not be able to avoid familiar people, who will make sure not to ask about my husband. They read newspapers. They know what's going on. Or they think they do.

But maybe I avoid them for exactly that reason. My husband, in bed with another man, a boy at that—where have I failed? Have I failed? Have I not offered my husband the pleasure a man should expect in marriage? Have I failed in my duties? There's plenty of infidelity in his circles, but none of it makes it into the papers or before a court of law, and as such that specific kind of infidelity doesn't exist. It does not exist because it remains privately indoors. In my case, with all this unwanted publicity, the cork has come off the bottle, so to speak, and that is not good. I will be *that woman,* a role I don't want to play.

So I'd better avoid these people's company. For now, anyway. Once the matter is past us, the financial problems sorted out, no one will look at me the wrong way. Money buys respect. What else is money good for?

10

The world is still hesitating between night and morning when I'm having breakfast. An early edition of a French newspaper (one of those intellectual pantheons that survived the war as well as the post-war purges while making as few concessions as possible), available here so early thanks to a nightly air connection between Paris and Venice, speaks of Italian railway and harbor strikes. It looks like a train to the Riviera is not an immediate option.

And no ferry either, from Genoa to Marseille, for example. I would not even be able to get to Genoa. Then what about a plane? I don't like the idea, even though airplanes have become quite comfortable in recent years. Nevertheless, I'm not a fan, mostly because I don't like getting locked up in a small space with a group of strangers for any duration. I came here by train, via France, Germany, and Austria, and of course in first class. That took me two days, but under the best possible conditions. Only the Italian railways are not yet up to scratch, but they are improving.

Oh well, I'll stay a few more days. I'll keep an eye on how things develop from a distance.

An elderly couple sits next to me. They speak Italian, and she says out loud and warningly to her husband: *A colazione non mangio uovo, bevo solo un café.*

I enjoy eating an omelet with toast and the black syrupy coffee they serve here. Nowhere outside Italy can I find such delicious coffee. Even in a simple bar on a street corner, frequented by manual laborers and low-level pen-pushers, the coffee is superior to anything I ever drank in Paris or Berlin.

The Bald Man is sitting a few tables away to my right, near one of the windows. He appears to be a guest at the hotel. Even now he ignores me, like all other guests do. He, however, ignores me not because I'm foreign but because he isn't here by chance. First in the restaurant, and now here. There's no coincidence. He is shadowing me, that's for sure.

I can find out his name without much trouble, or at least under what name he stays here, if I ask the right questions at the obliging young receptionists. Any good pretext would do. I'm a customer, rich, and a woman; they will not assume criminal intent with what sounds like an innocent question about another guest's identity.

But I'm not going to do anything at the moment. My need for revelation is not that urgent. I just want to have a few days free from conspiracies and mysteries. But it seems that's not going to happen.

After all, maybe The Bald Man's presence is a coincidence. There is such a thing as chance, I'm told. He has been staying here for several days, like a diplomat on a mission, and of course he eats out somewhere nearby when he is not dining at the hotel. I noticed him specifically because of his baldness. He ignores me because he is busy with other things—with his job, his assignment as a diplomat, whatever.

And yet. Call it intuition. It saved my life in the past.

After breakfast, I dress in inconspicuous clothes and head into town. I desperately need to see the main tourist attractions mentioned by poets and writers alike. I need to walk in their footsteps. This is probably the most written-about city in Europe, except perhaps for Paris. Venice is the subject of a vast library of novels, guidebooks, and picture books, all of which could take a single human life to read.

Well, a considerable number of them will probably be full of religious nonsense, not worth my time.

I figure out how to use the vaporetto, provide myself with sufficient tickets and a route planner (written in poor English), and off I go. I've heard that admiring Venice from the canals is a common practice, but this also applies to Paris and the Seine. In Paris, the Seine's low level makes it impossible to see much of the city. The situation is better here in Venice, especially because in many places the historical houses border directly on the canal.

I expect to hear from Edvardo again, him with his German diary. But he doesn't show up. I'm relieved, as I don't desire his trophy or need his problems.

I have a look at the Campo San Giacomo Dell'Orio, the pretentious Santa Maria Gloriosa dei Frari (and Titian's paintings), and the Mercato di Rialto (where I drink a chilled Valpolicella). Despite the cold weather, customers eat on the restaurant terraces or sit in the open windows of bars and small trattorias, many of them young and good-looking, comfortably dressed, sometimes even sloppily, all of them listening to American Jazz. This brings to mind Paris and its vibrant nightclubs and relaxed bars. Perhaps local writers and philosophers use to hang out in these bars and on the terraces here as well. I won't be familiar with their names and writing, a gap in my intellectual upbringing I'm all too aware of.

I have lunch—a salad and a glass of white wine—on a covered terrace, heated with artful but inefficient charcoal stoves. The roof over the terrace is a grid of wood, completely overgrown with ivy, the sort that remains green all year round. A young

Italian man in a splendid burgundy woolen overcoat reads an English copy of William Golding's *Lord of the Flies*.

I've read the book too—it's not particularly useful as an English language learning tool. However, an Italian who reads a book in any other language than his own deserves praise. They view Italian as a universal language, expecting all foreigners, including casual tourists, to speak it. Even a disastrous war does not dent their sense of superiority, which is utterly misplaced.

I spend the rest of the day as pleasantly as possible. The lawsuits in London are far from my mind. No, I'm lying. I think about my problems all the time, but there is no pressure and no obligation to do something about them right away. If Master Morse needs me, I will hear from him. And if necessary—even if against my will—I will take a plane to London at once.

11

Then, not unexpectedly, there's a telegram from Morse. He wanted to call me over the phone, he writes, but he couldn't reach the hotel, so he decided to send a cable instead. Sent from London last night. Delivered this morning for breakfast to my table, together with the strong steaming hot coffee and the almost artistically shaped rolls.

My pitiful husband has gone into hiding, a dismayed Morse informs me. For several days now, apparently. He has disappeared, gone up in smoke; nobody seems to know where he is. Morse inquires about my plans and whether I will return to London at the soonest so we can discuss this new and unwelcome development. My husband, hiding? In his case, that's not a good idea, according to Morse.

I will provide him with an answer, but not now. The hotel has its own telegraph desk, so I don't have to find a post office. I don't even know where there's a post office around here. Still, I'm not going to send a message right away. I need to sort things out for myself first. Will a court view my husband's hiding as evidence of his guilt? Perhaps this is an interesting development, and we should not simply let it pass us by. We have a certain leverage now, something we did not have before. I need Morse's advice on the situation.

But do I really need to return to London at once? Nothing seems really pressing, not even with this new situation. I might continue my exploration of Venice now that I'm here. Why should I feel obliged otherwise? However, can I act with the same carelessness as any ordinary visitor, understanding that certain developments in London require close monitoring?

Perhaps I should let Morse do the heavy lifting here. After all, he's my shield, my intermediary, my translator, the man who interprets all events for me, the man who turns intentions into actions, who convinces others of my innocence and my pitiful position, the man who points an accusing finger at others, claiming their property, money, and various possessions. My master Morse. I need not move; I need not intervene, not even now. Maybe he's not even expecting my answer to his query any time soon.

Nevertheless, I decide to respond. Once again on duty at the reception, the young and obliging Alberto produces a form in four languages, promising to send my missive by cable to the destination of my choice within the shortest possible time. My message to Morse is simple: I will wait a little longer before returning and count on him to keep me informed of developments. I don't need (or so I think, but I don't mention this) to make my life more complex than it already is, certainly not by returning to London, where lawyers from the opposing party, representatives of the Crown, and members of the press will undoubtedly not leave me in peace for even a moment. As the popular expression goes, I could do without their attention, like a toothache.

I then spend a few pleasant hours near Piazza San Marco. To the annoyance of the gondoliers, a dozen expensive private motor boats moor alongside the quay. The square itself is dry, with the obligatory pigeons being fed by a lonely but persistent old lady. She actually appears to be a compact pigeon herself.

A few weeks ago, twenty centimeters of water were covering the square and the surrounding alleys. People had to cross the square using narrow and hastily constructed bridges, little more than planks resting on stones. Not exactly conducive to tourism, but Venice lives its own stubborn life, slowly but elegantly sinking into the lagoon. The many bridges in the area bear witness to the precarious situation of this city, proof that it is less a structure than a kind of vessel, its inhabitants an indifferent crew, its doges admirals rather than city administrators.

I stop opposite La Fenice, the theater that burned down in 1836 but was subsequently rebuilt, a perfect replica of the original from the eighteenth century. Towards the end of the sixteenth century, the Arsenale, some distance away, was capable of constructing a warship in twelve hours if necessary. As it often was. In 1597 for example, a hundred ships were launched from this site in sixty days to keep the Turks away from Cyprus. The sixteen thousand workers with their cauldrons of boiling tar were an inspiration for Dante's seventh circle of hell. Today the complex is no longer accessible to tourists.

I am guided through the city by a Baedeker, without which many details of this former Republic would escape me. I am, however, only moderately interested in the past, which is rarely accessible any more.

Still, that past taught me valuable lessons in self-preservation. Literally. In the fields outside San Martino, I learned how to use a bayonet to defend myself against Germans and fascists, and a Welsh lieutenant showed me how to shoot a pistol and rifle, just in case. He even taught me how to fight unarmed, during which I learned to identify the weak spots of the human body. That kind of training was not compulsory, at least not for a civilian among their ranks, a journalist, and a woman at that—but the lieutenant judged that in the fray of battle, my gender and status could easily be overlooked. To him, a citizen with blood on her hands was better than a dead citizen. I am still grateful for his lessons.

A further account of my walk through the city may be of interest to the reader, but I have little to report that rises above the banal experience of the average tourist. No meetings with famous artists, prominent stars of the silver screen or politicians, or illustrious seducers. In November, night falls quickly, especially when the sky is overcast. The days are shortening, and at dusk the stubborn mist rises from the dark lagoon. The city comes to life, because there is money to be made, but I prefer sun-drenched beaches and cocktails under the shade of palms. I will probably be enjoying all of that soon. That is my aim at the moment. Endless beaches, endless hours of sun.

Edvardo, however, the man with the secret and the diary, disrupts my harmonic feelings, just as he thoroughly disrupts my plans. I don't know how he does it, but he manages to avoid the sharp eye of the receptionists and knocks on my door without further ado. Luckily I'm still dressed; it's almost seven, and I want to have dinner somewhere (if necessary in the hotel itself). I open the door, not expecting his appearance.

I immediately sense that something is amiss. He is barely able to stand upright. His legs could give out at any moment. First I suspect an advanced state of intoxication, then I assume an illness, and at last I stick to some violent encounter, God knows with whom. Someone, an enemy, has attacked him. I see no wounds, however, no blood.

"Signora Barth," he says, and his voice sounds fragile. "Signora Barth . . ." He extends his left hand (he holds himself upright against the door with the right) and hands me his accursed, and especially unwanted, manuscript. "Do you want to ensure that this ends up with the right people?"

"I can't . . ." I begin, but he cuts me off right away, likely anticipating my objections.

"I'm not selling it; I'm giving it to you. You are my only, my last hope. It must reach the most appropriate people, who will then proceed to make its content public. They must! So many prominent figures are mentioned in here, and most of them have not seen trial in Nuremberg. For political reasons, the prosecutor refrained from utilizing all the information at his disposal. No, I'm not coming in. You are already at risk. They may have seen me . . . Those names—these are people who today still belong to the political elite and the ruling class, both in Germany and elsewhere. They managed to escape their fate at that time. That shouldn't happen again."

He glances over his shoulder in the hallway. I follow his gaze. The hallway is empty.

"Do you promise me . . ?"

Promise him something? What should I promise him? That I'm going to take care of his bloody diary? That I will be the messenger of his last wishes? I do not intend to give my word to a man I barely know. "I'll see what I can do," I admit cautiously. "But can't we better involve the police?"

I have the cardboard folder in both hands now. He releases his grip and retreats. The police won't be an option. "Thank you," he whispers, and he hurries back down the hall as fast as his weakened state allows. He disappears behind a corner.

I'm here now, part of yet another vague, almost intangible plot. This plot has no connection to me. It is a conspiracy that other people have set in motion and into which I am drawn against my will, at the hands of a man I cannot really rely on but who trusts me for reasons still unclear.

I don't want any part in this. I don't want to be part of this adventure. I have enough on my plate without having to worry about an obscure conspiracy by, with, or against fascist powers. I don't want anything to do with politics, especially not this kind.

Solutions are obvious: I destroy the manuscript, or I take it to the police. But in both cases, I will have failed. I will have failed, especially in a moral sense. Not that I have any obligation towards Edvardo. I do have an obligation, however, to my fellow countrymen and to all others who died in order to eradicate fascism. It is a cancer that has spread throughout human society. Large pieces of that cancer have now been cut away, but lumps here and there still remain, and however small they may be today, they will eventually fester and grow and poison humanity once again. Therefore, I must utilize the manuscript in the manner suggested by Edvardo. If Nazi accomplices persist, even within the political salons of European capitals, we must expose and eliminate them.

12

That night, no grotesque Nazi assassin forces himself into my room and slits my throat. No team of SAS officers tie me up and make off with the diary. No immoral collectors of Nazi memorabilia are waiting for me in the hallway, with grabby hands and open wallets. None of that. I have carefully hidden the diary between my clothes, an idiotic, completely undignified, and ineffective hiding place, but for the time being I have no other solution. Whoever wants it can have it. Yes, I am aware of my moral obligation. However, I also want to live my own life. How do I combine these ambitions?

I rush through the lavish breakfast and am about to leave the slightly overcrowded restaurant when the maître stops me. "Signora Bart," he says, a little breathlessly, "a call from London." He leads me to an ornate mahogany booth in a discreet corner, where he hands me the receiver of a wall telephone. I say my name.

It's Morse. A familiar but distant voice. He says, "Mrs. Barth," in the pedantic tone I've come to expect from him, a tone he also uses in court, usually to considerable effect. "I feel it would be a good idea if you stayed in Venice a while longer. The press over here is showing just a little too much interest in your case.

Certain unsavory details have unfortunately been leaked, and everyone involved is being held accountable. I myself and my office have declined to make any sort of statement, and neither will your husband's family. However, your sudden appearance in the capital will not exactly go unnoticed, and all the pressure might end up on your shoulders. For the time being, you are sufficiently safe in Venice. You can stay safe in Venice as long as you steer clear of the press, and the Italians show no concern for our cause."

"Why would they do that?"

"I'm afraid, Mrs. Barth, the press is the same everywhere. A juicy story always means more newspaper copies sold. These reporters have a tendency to write captivating pieces with poignant titles, which may not always align with the truth. Almost never, actually."

"I haven't noticed any interest in my person as yet," I say. Do I mention my persistent visitor and the manuscript? No, I don't. It would only complicate the whole affair. And Morse probably can't help me with that story, or so I assume.

"I can only advise you," he continues, "to be discreet and avoid the press. Also, don't speak to anyone who seems suspicious."

Well, I thoroughly messed up that last item. I have the feeling I have spoken to nothing but suspicious individuals so far. Regardless, I have no desire to share with Morse the details of Edvardo and the Nazi executioner's diary. The whole subject should remain safely confined to Venice.

"Meanwhile, your husband's photo appears in the newspapers, and his family calls on him to make himself heard. But I suspect all of this will prove useless. He will now avoid public life more than ever before. Maybe he's trying to escape abroad. All this plays to our advantage, of course."

"When will the case come to trial?" I inquire.

"Oh, I'm afraid it will be a few weeks before the public hearings start. You understand that no-one here wants to rush or force the administration of justice. The question is whether the young man in question, whom we discussed, remains willing to testify. That is still our main concern at this point."

"You have my testimony. I caught them in bed."

"Of course. And it will be a very . . . graphic testimony, I'm sure. But you are an involved party. As I previously explained, this complicates the situation further. The court will take partiality into account. On the other hand, you have an impeccable reputation."

An impeccable reputation. He doesn't know what I did at the Ritz and other expensive London hotels before the war. No one who knows me today is aware of that part of my past. At least that's what I hope. I hope someone doesn't suddenly show up—a former customer who recognizes me on photos and such. Should that happen, my impeccable reputation would abruptly crumble. Consequently, my legal case may no longer be in its optimal condition.

"Anyhow," he continues, unaware of my doubts, "an additional testimony is essential for us. Almost indispensable even. So we need the young man."

"Weren't you planning on getting him caught? My husband, I mean. In the act?"

"That is of course no longer possible, because we don't know where he is."

Well, a missed opportunity, I guess. It was a nice plan. But that's the way it is with appealing plans: they rarely survive the first confrontation with the enemy.

"So I'm going to hang around here for a while longer."

"If you don't mind. You can also go somewhere else. France, the Riviera, Paris. Any place where you can remain anonymous.

If possible, try not to travel or book a hotel room under your own name. And you might also want to stay away from public events, and wherever there are photographers around."

He drives me crazy with his spy adventures. How can I book a train ticket under a name other than my own?

We say goodbye. I promise to keep him informed of my movements. He promises to keep me informed on the progress in the case. My husband's relatives haven't been in contact with him, he finally tells me. They are undoubtedly aware of the problems waiting for them in and beyond the court hearings. Even with my husband gone missing, they will face various demands for compensation, all of them perfectly detailed by Morse. All of which suits me just fine.

13

I now return to the past for a moment. I have to. I am not free from the past. London, 1939. The man holding open the door to the drawing room had a gleaming bald scalp as if he never had hair, and the eyelids of an Asian, which perhaps he was. You may have seen men like him in those Fu Manchu films, but they were portrayed by American or British actors with a bad accent, heavy make-up, and fake nails. He bowed to us, the Chinese on duty; he bowed to me and to the gentleman who accompanied me (or who was accompanied by me, depending on the interpretation of the facts). Then, behind us, he closed the door again, leaving us all alone in the drawing room.

And what kind of drawing room that was. I was familiar with the fantasies of pseudo-romantics who saw turn-of-the-century France as the pinnacle of Western civilization, and thus needed deep armchairs, usually upholstered in dark red velvet, lots of gilded stuff, indirect light, and draperies behind which an army of servants or maidens could remain hidden. Hunting scenes and stern-looking portraits hung against the silk wallpaper, and an open bar with the best brands of Cognac and Single Malt. On a coffee table, an open box of cigars, a silver lighter, and crystal ashtray (my companion did not smoke, however). During those years, every large hotel in London offered a few of these drawing rooms for rent, either by the hour or by the evening, thereby transforming vice into a lucrative business.

This was the early spring of 1939, a sad year for humanity. However, many sad years would follow, and many years would challenge my belief in humanity's values.

The year marked the end of Europe's peace, which later transformed into a fictitious conflict, a diplomatic charade. As the drums pounded and the rigid arms raised, the slaughter of Jews and other minorities, along with intellectuals and communists, continued, and the notion of perpetual peace was a belief only held by the foolish.

The man who entered the salon with me was not one of those fools, and he certainly did not believe in world peace. Instead, he made huge profits selling military equipment to various countries that would, one day, be at war with each other. He boasted of his industrial genius, which is why I knew about his professional activities. He had plenty of money, and if he wanted, he could simply have bought me, whatever my price would have been.

He didn't want to buy me; he wanted to rent me for the evening. I saw hunger in his eyes, but not for food. These kinds of men have never known ordinary hunger.

Until that moment, I had been his invité, his dinner guest, but now it was past midnight, and at his request he transformed me into something else, an inhabitant of the deep ravine of the night, the complex object of his desire. Over the past few hours, he treated me courteously at the table and afterwards over the cognac, showcasing his sophistication as a man of the world capable of impressing any woman, even if he paid me for this role. None of those gentlemen had their legitimate wives accompanying them; it was all an act. All the girls in the group were hired. Some, I suspected, were still minors.

Neither the police nor the courts would ever hear about any of this. Money mutilates: witnesses, especially the staff who served the guests and ourselves, suddenly became deaf and blind when inquired about the events of evenings such as those.

There was no bed in the salon, but there were a number of spacious armchairs and imposing sofas, making every physical excess possible. From experience, I took a wait-and-see attitude: did he want me to undress right away, or was he going to do my undressing? Did he also want to be undressed, or would he rather not? Did he want to take me missionary style or doggy style?

Did he want to hurt me, or did he want to be inflicted with pain? Was humiliation his privilege, or did he want to humiliate? Much was possible, although it stopped at permanent mutilation because I still had to live off my body later. All men were supposed to understand this, but sometimes they mistakenly believed they were superior to all other masters. I knew a couple of girls who barely had a face left and no one to help them survive. But these were the exceptions.

Yet you ran a certain risk at every opportunity.

Most of the time, the focus was on humiliation rather than pain. These men, who were willing to go to extreme lengths, had no interest in inflicting pain on their victims. No, they wanted to humiliate them because they hated women—all women, especially their wives.

But what they could not do to the wife, did not dare to do to their spouse, they did to the anonymous, hired girls. All of us knew it and had been humiliated, but only a few were permanently disfigured. However, we all tore our souls apart, without exception. You don't see a soul, however. It may tear. No one will notice when it tears open. You can move on with a mutilated soul, but not with a mutilated face.

14

My preferred feeling, my beloved status, the circumstance I most long for, is solitude. I freely admit, when questioned, I prefer to be alone. I don't need people around me all the time, maybe not even at all. They bother me with their presence. They prevent me from thinking clearly. Everything they do, clouds my mind.

However, imagine wishing to be alone in the midst of a war as you struggle to survive on a battlefield, perhaps in a recently liberated but nearly destroyed village, or on a road surrounded by troops, all while knowing you urgently need to write a story for your newspaper. No way you're granted a morsel of solitude. There are always people around, or at least some evidence of human life, such as explosions, shouted orders, and passing vehicles. Life is depressingly present. It is categorically impossible to experience loneliness in the middle of one of modern humanity's greatest stories—a story that would later be the subject of hundreds of books and films.

Yet there I am. It's mid-1944, and Italy is unlike anything tourists have ever experienced. Italy doesn't even exist anymore. It has largely become a hell that Dante would recognize. In a dirty corner of what used to be a terraced house in what remains of

70

a village, I lean against a wall, studying the blood spatter on the sleeve of my khaki jacket. The stripes and insignia have been torn off the jacket because, as a civilian correspondent, I am not allowed to wear a uniform. I have just shot and killed a German soldier with a Garand rifle at a distance of a mere two meters. It's his blood on the jacket. I tried to revive him, even though I had blown off half his head. It's absurd; I realize it now, and I realized it while I was doing it, but inside me there was only the will to put right what I had ruined: a human life.

He was my second victim. A week earlier, I drove a bayonet into the belly of an Italian fascist sergeant who wanted to rape me. Although covered in dirt and blood, he looked even younger than I. He was naive rather than cruel, rash rather than malicious, and above all, he was desperate. He saw a woman under my dirty clothes, and he wanted to forget the war for a moment. He did not see the bayonet that I carried with me, to defend myself against men like him.

It remains remarkable how slowly a person dies and how much time it can take, even for a man whose head has been half blown off. The rest of the body doesn't realize it is dead and is still occupied planning the future and clinging to banal, everyday functions. Bleeding to death from an abdominal wound takes even longer, but eventually all hope disappears with the blood. The Italian sergeant lay there in his dirty black uniform, his pants still around his hips. He tried to stop the blood with his hands, but in his eyes I saw he knew. He knew that shortly afterwards I would be lonely again.

In North Africa, places to hide were hard to find. Most of the time, you made do with old, historical ruins left behind by cultures that no longer had names. And then there was the desert itself, frighteningly empty. So much for choice. The war took place largely in the desert, far away from cities or any decent-sized settlements. Troops marched, tanks and trucks battled against the sand and the heath, shedding blood and causing bodies to fall, either intact or in pieces, under a rain of bullets or metal shards. The sand then covered everything again, as it had done for centuries. The remains of entire civilizations have sunk into the deep vault that is the Sahara, and so did proof of our own times. Waging war seemed easy there, or so I thought at first—but the desert offered nothing—no shelter, no water, no shade, no compassion. Italy is different because there is a comforting, sometimes excessive nature, and buildings, which are proof of human pride and endeavor.

But, strangely enough, in Italy I longed for the endless dunes. I wanted to be alone again, like I had been in the desert. The mostly empty horizon invites you to immerse yourself in its infinity. There's even too much horizon. Even in the company of people, you only need to take a few steps and you find yourself in the empty nothingness, away from civilization, surrounded by reddish or brown sand and boulders or an almost white salt flat—and there's nothing, nothing else but absolute quiet.

We crossed the sea on board of a stinking freighter, eyes on the skies even when we knew air superiority had been regained by the Allies. I followed in the footsteps of British, American, and Canadian forces and found myself in some sad and nameless port, all cracked concrete and stained steel, with a total lack of amenities. Just over the green hills, Germans and Italians were waiting for us. The Allied planes were masters of the sky, but no one was master over Italian soil except death.

I imagined I could only be alone on the Italian front if I shot everyone around me, and such a radical initiative would then surely end the war as well. But I wasn't there to kill people, although I eventually did. I was there to report about killings done by others. I had to write about the glory and the heroics, about the commitment of the Allied troops and the treachery of The Enemy, and that was what I did best.

And so I wrote personal stories about soldiers who had done extraordinary things. None of them regarded themselves as heroes. It was, to most of them, a job to be done, as quickly as possible and without getting hurt or killed. That's what most of my stories were about, at least the ones I wrote during those first months in North Africa. In the desert, people assumed they could rise above themselves. They all want to be the next T.E. Lawrence. Many succumbed to romance's breathless disease. Quite a few soldiers and officers I had met suffered from that disease. Some died as a result.

In the desert, every human act has meaning; there is little room for interpretation. Life and death and all that—it's all neatly defined. There is also a clear ideological demarcation: a strict boundary between what we are and what the enemy is. We are civilization, and the enemy clearly is not. Between the two lies a wide, even impassable strip of desert.

In Italy, that border was unclear. Italians fought on the side of the Nazis, and other Italians fought on the side of the Allies, and still other Italians did not fight at all. Poles not only fought on our side, but also served in the German army, including the Waffen SS. Italian civilians were massacred by the Nazis. The same thing happened on our side, too. It became more difficult to distinguish heroes from psychopaths. It became more difficult to distinguish selfless acts from madness. Everything became more difficult. However, I could write whatever I wanted, as long as it passed the censors' scrutiny. If necessary, I also wrote about victims, deaths, failure, and suffering. What I couldn't write about was the absurdity of the war, because I had no words for it.

15

The Bald Man makes his appearance once again later in the day, while I have just left the San Giacomo dell'Orio, where I have been admiring Veronese's paintings. He's waiting for me at the bottom of the stairs, and this time he brazenly reveals that he's here for me. "Scusami, Signora," he says politely, and he immediately continues in elegant and almost accent-free English. "There is some matter of mutual concern we need to discuss. My name is Van Rijn, and I am interested in rare historical objects that have a certain economic value precisely because of their rarity. Maybe I can buy you a coffee."

The urgent look and the contrasting polite words persuade me not to refuse his proposal. And of course, I am curious; otherwise, I wouldn't have just gone along with him.

The nearby bar where we enter tries to make people forget about the past war by combining glass and steel with a worn and therefore authentic counter, as well as the usual collection of bottles against the mirror wall. The lighting is indirect and discreet.

Two coffees at a table in the back. Then he speaks again. "I have no intention of misleading you, Signora," he carefully says. "You have a document in your possession that my clients have a specific interest in, and they are willing to pay handsomely for it. I'm talking about a considerable sum."

There we are: another interested party. How does he know about me having the manuscript? "Maybe I should first hear from you who those clients are, Mr. Van Rijn." Because of his name, I suspect he is Dutch, or has Dutch roots. He has, however, no Dutch accent at all. Rather, he sounds like he was born somewhere in Central Europe. "I am not willing to discuss matters of money with people I do not know."

He makes a gesture that should indicate his modest role. "I am at most an intermediary. But even in this guise, I can still act independently, at least to a certain extent. However, this also means that I must treat all information regarding my clients with the uttermost discretion. As such, I won't mention any names. The price we are willing to pay for the object in your possession is all that matters to you."

"And that object is . . ."

"Well, the diary, ma'am, of course."

This is an odd and uncomfortable situation. Why didn't he negotiate with Edvardo? Or did he already do that, resulting in Edvardo's miserable condition? Was violence used during that encounter? If I choose not to cooperate, will they use violence against me? I see a potential danger in this man. He seems civilized enough, but that's just the outer layer. Underneath lies something I don't want to know. I am having coffee with him in a Venetian café, but that's as far as I am willing to take this relationship.

There is no point in denying that I have the diary. He knows. How he knows is irrelevant. This is not a diplomatic game. There are more than just financial interests involved. The amount his clients are willing to spend on the diary and related papers is a mere detail. I ask for anything, and as long as my price is not exorbitant, they will agree to do business with me. The diary itself has no value for them. Its non-existence has value, at least to the people I suspect to be behind this encounter. They will destroy it or make sure it no longer sees the light of day.

Let me free myself from my burden. Would that not be a good idea? I ask him for a reasonable amount of money, and he gets the diary. Then I can focus on more important matters, personal matters. My future, more specifically. I'm not a moral person. What do I care if a number of Nazis get away with whatever they did and keep on cherishing their black ideology into old age? What do I care if, ten years after the war, they still hold high positions in certain ministries and government offices in that depressing country of theirs? I really should not care one bit.

However, I was not a casual witness to the war. I was—and am—not a passerby in history. And that's why the dairy and its content really matter to me. Three weeks after their liberation, I visited the camps. The bodies had been cleared away, and the surviving prisoners largely evacuated. But the mass graves, the ovens, the gas chambers, and some witnesses were still there. The smell was still there. The dark earth, the charred remains. I don't feel responsible for the dead, nor am I to blame for the atrocities. I feel responsible towards the living and towards memory. I wrote my best pieces about responsibility during those two years at the end of the war and just after the surrender, articles and reports that established my reputation.

Van Rijn is old enough to have himself been a witness. He may have actively experienced the war. But maybe his story is very different from mine. However, I suspect he is not a moral person either. He may have incurred debts in some form during the war and is now paying them off. Wrong debts, with the wrong people. After the victims were buried, he now also wants to bury the evidence against the guilty.

And I'm not going to help him do that.

"I'm afraid, Mr. Van Rijn, I can't help you," I say.

That clearly doesn't go over well, although he could have expected my decision.

"Really?" he says. As if he's throwing me one last lifeline.

"I'm sorry," I say. But of course I'm not sorry.

"This may turn out to be a mistake, Mrs. Barth," he says, in a mocking tone that leaves little to my imagination. "The price my clients are willing to offer certainly outweighs your inability to see the true meaning and importance of the diary."

"My inability . . ."

"It should be no more than a commodity to you. Something you want to get rid of at a profit. I'm offering you ten thousand dollars in cash. That's certainly enough, isn't it? I assume that you will not let such a sum, a princely sum, I dare say, pass you by."

The amount is indeed significant, and despite my current financial situation, I can put that money to good use. But why would I now exchange for money something that was given to me for free? Have I suddenly become ethical? No, not in the least. An obscure offer like this suggests a higher value. He offers ten thousand. Someone else could offer a lot more.

So I refuse. The farewell is abrupt and not entirely amicable.

16

I expect Edvardo's body to be found by the local police any moment now, somewhere in one of the canals or in the lagoon. A dramatic but fitting end to what was undoubtedly a remarkable life. I'm trying to decipher the local newspaper, but as far as I can tell, there's no mention of a body that could be his. This city seems blissfully crime-free. I have heard that this is an illusion, but police and city officials conspire to keep most forms of crime hidden from the outside world, and in particular from emerging tourism. Journalism also contributes to this cover-up—in exchange for what, I don't know.

Gossip, however, is plentiful in the press: about film stars and starlets surprised during potentially embarrassing activities; about wealthy real estate agents involved in construction violations and outright scams; about self-enriching politicians; about industrialists and other famous people whose reputations are to be thoroughly ruined without the city being endangered. There's a rule that everything happening elsewhere, in other major cities around the country, can be exposed at will and without restraint. The Venetian press repeatedly attacks local politicians from Rome and Milan, to name just two cities. Dragged through the mud, as it were. Even today, these cities continue to engage in age-old feuds. But local politicians are to be spared as much as possible.

I continue my exploration through the city. Every building and every square has its own story to tell. Consider the San Lorenzo church on Campo S. Lorenzo. Renaissance aristocrats, who did not want or could not spend money on their daughters' dowries, dismissed the girl in question to this place, which for centuries had been a monastery. The girls had no say in the process at all. However, the young nuns, who knew they could not leave the monastery ever again, ended up being notorious for not acting very obedient to the decency rules of both church and society. They decided for themselves what their rules and freedoms should be. Only the imagination offers a limit to what that meant, as they knew very little restraint in their sexual practices. At one point, the situation became so severe that the Patriarch of Venice had the monastery's gate nailed shut so that no more male visitors could pass through. The noble nuns then set fire to the gate. This goes to show that women did not always play a subordinate role, certainly not in this society. And good for them.

Marco Polo was buried here, so the story goes, but his earthly remains were lost when the church was renovated at the end of the sixteenth century. Further on, in San Zulian's facade stands the statue of the scientist and patron of the arts, Tommaso Rangone, who became known for a book in which he explained how a person could easily reach the blessed age of one hundred and twenty. However, when he himself died at the young age of eighty, he lost his readership.

I'm now a long way from my hotel in the eastern part of the city, thanks to the efficient vaporettos that take me more or less in comfort from one place to another. It is, in a way, like the Underground in London. The difference is that the quality of the air experienced here in Venice is better, even while traveling. Just like the view.

These trips around town lend me the opportunity to check whether I am being followed. Does someone follow me, observing and monitoring my every action? Suspicion was instilled in me as a child and has proven useful many times afterwards. I don't see anyone displaying more than a passing interest in my person. However, I am inexperienced in these types of situations and expect spies to act professionally and expertly (and therefore remain invisible). But who would shadow me, and why? Someone hired by Van Rijn's clients?

Time slowly flows by, much like the water in the canals. This is Venice, after all, where history is a matter of centuries and where the state archives on the Rio Terra S. Toma are thirty-six miles long and go back a thousand years, far beyond the capacity of human memory. Maybe I'll add the infamous diary to these archives. However, I have placed the folder in my new personal safe at a bank, where the director, upon spotting my checkbook, provided fast and efficient service without any questions. That's exactly how I left the love letters written by my husband in a safe in London. There's no key involved here, just a numerical code. If I die unexpectedly, this vault will only be opened in fifty years and its secrets revealed to a by then indifferent society. I do not believe in an afterlife or any form of eternal existence, and therefore I will not care about the fate of those documents after my death.

I used to read quite a few books about Venice, including the infamous novel by Ernest Hemingway, who, as a middle-aged man, found a young mistress here. I quickly discarded his rather mediocre book in favor of more sensible nineteenth-century historical material. So many writers tried to give meaning to their lives, or to understand the universe, by dedicating their labor and their creativity to words, characters, and fiction. That's how emerged a romantic image of this city. However, the real Venice is far more captivating than any imagined version. Historical characters have a much richer dimension than those who are merely fictional. Take the monk Giustinian, who in 1172 was the only one of his family left after a maritime disaster. The Pope, mindful of the inevitable fate of the almost completely lost family line, temporarily released him from his celibacy vows in order to marry a daughter of the Doge. Over the following years, the monk diligently produced twelve descendants, who would hold important positions in the city, as did their descendants, for centuries to come. What writer would come up with such a story?

Definitely not me. But then again, I'm not very good in the imagination department. I couldn't write a novel or even a short story. But then again, I'm proficient at conspiracies. I'm skilled at weaving illusions.

17

The young man at the hotel reception—not Alberto but a colleague of his, equally young and fresh from hotel school, I assume—frowns at me, as if my mere presence constitutes an insult all on itself, to Venice and to the whole of Italy. The reason for this cold reception soon becomes clear: two gentlemen are discreetly waiting for me in a salon, and they belong to the police force. Not the one who directs traffic, but the real police, who investigate serious crimes.

That's what they tell me, or at least one of them tells me— the older of the two, whose face is marred by a scar across his left cheek. His name is Inspector Martinengo, and he does not introduce his younger colleague. Inspector Martinengo speaks English, which is why he is here, because in Italian, this interview would be much more difficult, take much longer, and require the services of an official translator. I simply leave him in the dark about my admittedly limited knowledge of his language.

"Signora Barth," he says, after the succinct introduction, "you are here as a tourist, I presume? To visit the city, am I right? Want to see the lovely places? You want to relish and appreciate history and everything else?"

"That's correct, inspector," I admit. I resolve to only answer his questions, not elaborate on details. Avoid sharing unsolicited information. He can get a yes and a no. And I understand, a hotel like this does not like to have police visiting its premises, especially not to interrogate one of its guests. That doesn't look good. Reputation is damaged easily enough in this sector.

"You were here before the war, correct? Here in Venice, I mean."

"Indeed, I was."

"Mmmm. You are also here on your own. Alone, I mean." It is not a question, but an observation, and it sounds like he disapproves of a woman traveling without a male companion. Furthermore, he dislikes a culture that allows women to travel on their own, particularly to his city, where he has to keep things in order because of all those women running loose.

I don't fall into his trap and just say, in a friendly and polite tone (which, by the way, requires a special effort on my part): "That's right, inspector, I'm traveling on my own." So, the mutual positions are perfectly clear from the start. He thinks I'm an upstart and a problem, and I don't like his attitude.

"Such is of course not prohibited, Signora. Not by any law." He coughs briefly, as if the idea bothers him. There should be a law allowing him to arrest me on the spot. "But why do you travel alone and not with your husband?"

Right now, I can tell him that it's none of his bloody business. That traveling alone is not against any law; that I am a free citizen of a free country; that my passport and visa are in order; and that it is not the police's business whether I travel alone here or in any other country. I want to tell him as much, and yet I don't. Because those Italians are fond of their self-esteem, let's call it that for lack of anything better. Self-esteem. An Italian man does not recognize a woman as equal. Such was not the case a hundred years ago, and neither is it now. Don't expect them to change. Unless, on some highly exceptional occasion, the woman happens to be a movie star or an opera singer. Then she is treated with consideration that even surpasses that received by her male counterparts. I, however, do not find myself within such a category. I am a nobody. Therefore, people suspect me of committing an unspecified breach of civility by traveling without my spouse.

"My husband and I are going through a divorce," I explain.

He continues to look at me impassively. By confirming my divorce situation, I am probably making my case worse. I haven't asked, but I suspect that in this old-fashioned Catholic country, divorce is not exactly an option, and couples are doomed to live together forever. Like him with his own wife. Maybe he wants to be away from her, but he can't. So in his eyes, I am a sinful woman, but at the same time, I am a challenge. I possess an unthinkable form of freedom.

"Divorce," he says, and for a brief moment he glances at the young policeman, who doesn't respond. "You're getting divorced, and you're traveling alone. Far away from home."

"That's right, Inspector."

He probably expects this kind of behavior from the French. An inherently sinful people. And unreliable too. But a British lady like me? No, he did not expect any of that from the British. However, I remain convinced that he already knew about my background, the divorce, and such. He did not arrive here unprepared. Would not have, I'm sure. And so I wonder why he's here at all and why I'm here.

"What exactly do you want from me, Inspector?" I inquire. In this case, attack seems the best defense, as that lieutenant once explained to me while demonstrating how to defend myself with blank weapons and bare hands. Always strike where the enemy doesn't expect it and where he's weakest. Taking advantage of the enemy's ignorance. It's an old strategy, always effective.

"The British police," he continues, with an undertone of suppressed annoyance that matches the subject, "contacted our offices, asking to find out how long you have been here and whether you are still here. They seem worried by your husband's disappearance."

From the perspective of the British police, it is already considered a disappearance. Interesting. It is no longer a matter of hiding, although in practice the distinction would be subtle. What distinguishes one disappearing person from any other who disappears voluntarily? What makes each case different? This is a problem that I do not wish to solve in the current context.

"The disappearance of my husband," I repeat thoughtfully. I lure him onward to further explanations. I won't meet him, not even halfway. He gets paid to investigate, and he will not get a helping hand from me.

He frowns, clearly annoyed. He doesn't like me playing this game, not with him. But because we converse in a language that isn't his, he has no real strategy for dealing with my delays. "It is indeed a disappearance, madam. Your husband is missing. He can no longer be found."

His English even reaches into the overarching jungle of synonymous descriptions. Well done. This deserves a moment of my humble respect. An applause, but a silent one.

"Perhaps he no longer *desires* to be located," I speculate. "Then this is not a disappearance. He went into hiding. I seem to recall my lawyer using similar terminology."

"So you know about his . . . absence."

"Indeed. I am aware of his absence." And then I remain silent again. I am aware. There's nothing more to it. He is a detective, so he is very capable of drawing the wrong conclusions.

"Why would your husband go into hiding?"

"You know we are involved in a lawsuit, my husband and I? The divorce? Which is not exactly amicable?"

"Amicable?"

"Friendly."

"Ah," he says, but he doesn't elaborate on what he knows or doesn't know.

"My husband committed an indiscretion . . . with another man," I clarify. I succumb to the temptation of providing excessive details. But hey, I assume Inspector Martinengo is also aware of this detail. And a relationship between men is what those Italians are familiar with, isn't it? Despite the suffocating grip of the Catholic Church and fascism (whether in the past or not), homosexuality is less of an unsavory taboo here in his country than in mine. By the way, we are quite close to Greece, and they invented *that.* Or didn't they?

"Relationship," he says, tasting the word. I suspect he wants to taste each of my words and appreciate them. "Relationship," he says again. "And that's why he . . . went into hiding?"

"Because he runs the risk of being punished for such a behavior, Inspector. In my country, it is a serious offense. Against the law. Indecency, I think it is called."

"Yes, I realize that," says the inspector. His companion, who is barely old enough to shave, remains unmoved. He's here as a witness. To what? What must he testify to? I still suspect he doesn't understand a word of the entire conversation. That must be frustrating. Not quite much of a witness, isn't he?

However, this is not my problem. I have to concentrate on the inspector, who clearly holds no sympathy for me and my situation. Me and my cheating gay husband. This case undoubtedly confirms the inspector's prejudices—as held by many Italians— that the British are weak, decadent, unreliable, and not really Europeans, even though thousands gave their lives to help free this country from fascism. Let me even add this: Italians are not soldiers at all, not heroic fighters at all, and on their own they would not have defeated their right-wing compatriots and the Nazis. No, that is grossly unfair to the thousands of brave partisans who died during the war. It's a prejudice, I realize: I've seen brave Italians and cowardly Brits.

But let's stick to the matter at hand.

"You've been here the past few days? All the time?" he inquires. He mentions the date of my arrival. I confirm. And yes, I was everywhere, mostly visiting the city.

He gets uncomfortable. His mission, this interrogation, is basically pointless. My soon-to-be ex-husband, who is clearly innocent of any wrongdoing, is evading British justice while I'm here in Venice, and that's what he and his assistant are spending their time on. I wonder if an investigating judge ordered my interrogation. Most likely, someone wanted to do the British police or the consulate a favor. Should I tell him about Edvardo and his treacherous diary? About Van Rijn? No, I'm not going to do that. I'm not going to make my life more complicated than it already is.

18

None of the men I interacted with in London in the late 1930s—professionally, I mean—knew who I was, knew my true name, or learned anything about my family. I used a variety of names as best suited me. None of those names were suggestive or even exotic, unlike the names that later became common in the profession. Me and the other girls (I only knew a handful, and none of which I got to know well or intimately) used monickers like Anne, Gabriele, Deirdre, Jenny, or Sophie, and sometimes we were Desiree or Gwen. Everything but our real names. We did not keep our bodies for ourselves, but we did keep our identity.

On top of living anonymously and receiving our earnings solely in cash (due to the lack of bank accounts for ordinary citizens in those years), we only knew the men by names that were a far cry from their true identities as well. I got into the habit of calling them all Samuel in my mind because I didn't want to make any distinctions. As a result, they did not have a personality of their own, and I did not become attached to any of them, although I would occasionally meet the same man two or three times. I longed to disappear behind the screen of decency, secretly ashamed of my actions. Fortunately, someone granted me a means of disappearance, but only after I had earned enough to advance my future in other directions.

One Samuel was not the other. Their desires and the rewards were not the same. From our first conversation, I quickly learned to judge men by details—by a glance, by a single gesture. By the looks and the shape of their mouths, and the words they spoke. I learned a lot that I would later put to good use.

We kept our interactions with the other girls to a minimum, communicating only to warn about potential men. No one protected us; we had no pimp or agent, we all worked independently. We heard stories about pimps and agents, but these moved in different environments and usually catered to clients slightly lower on the social ladder than ours. The men we came into contact with did not care much for, nor did they need, those kinds of intermediaries. Such intermediaries could not set foot in the hotels where we worked. We were, so to speak, the High Society of the escort service. Thanks to this thin layer of glamour, we kept ourselves sane and safe.

Part of our income went to the staff at the hotels where we worked. Our discretion was of course theirs, and even their management shared in our earnings; otherwise, it would have been impossible for us to work. We would have had to take our business to clubs or bars—unsavory places where we would have had to compete with the girls who worked for pimps, coppers, and the like. The rough trade, so to speak. And soon enough we would have found ourselves in the same position as them, in other words: unenviable. But luckily, everyone involved in the posh hotel business appreciated a handful of banknotes on a regular basis.

Nevertheless, we had to act discreetly. We could not possibly hang out at the bar of one of the better hotels, even though we dressed as conventionally as possible. A woman simply did not venture by herself in such a place, not in those days. We usually made agreements through a network we had set up ourselves. It mainly consisted of our customers advertising us to friends, colleagues, and their own customers. Our individual reputation was our best and often only form of advertising. We weren't going to place an ad on the pages of The Times.

This course of action also protected us from the other persistent danger: the police. British society was permeated by a suffocating conventionality in which everyone knew his or her place and stayed there. There was no fishing or hunting outside the marriage—although these activities did occur frequently enough. Only those with money could afford the indulgences that accompanied potential exposure. It was not our gentlemen-customers who would be in danger, but us, who had no form of protection whatsoever. No lawyer would think of defending us in court.

In that respect, British society had not changed fundamentally since the Victorian era. Anyone who had aspirations to climb the social ladder had to meet a number of strict conditions: you had to be a man, of course, from a good family (a noble title was an extra advantage), wealthy, and you had to respect your superiors. Sex was only a necessity in marriage, and any woman still ran a considerable risk of pregnancy in the hope of giving birth to a son. A son, indeed. A male heir.

These men were no different from any other men in the long and painful history of the human species. They wanted to reproduce, and more specifically, have sons. They also wanted to expend their energy through sex, but not necessarily with their wives. There was a reason why a number of men went to the colonies, especially if they were single: exotic girls and women. The colonies offered less regulation, fewer restrictions, and an almost limitless pool of seductive locals. Or so these men assumed. Reality would soon catch up with them.

An older generation came to us with their needs. The women, dressed in blue stockings, were worn out, constricted, and fearful of losing their status, which prevented them from engaging in excess. On the other hand, the men continued to believe they were virile, despite the fact that they were usually not (we had a few aids and potions to remedy this, and lying also worked). Every Samuel who crossed my path desired the treatment he rightfully deserved, yet which his wife refused to grant. I suspect this game has been going on since humans became self-aware.

For more than two years, this was my working environment; this was my world. During the day, I was a diligent student, living in a rather shabby room with a landlady. She would join me after five with a bottle of Port, which I was more than happy to supply, sometimes stolen from a hotel stock. She never noticed how my travel bag, which I left at dusk (or earlier, depending on the season), was well-filled, containing my evening clothes, because I couldn't go out on the street dressed professionally. I could come back at any time, even in the morning, while the landlady slept off her stupor.

That particular world shriveled, capsized, and disappeared from view when, in the spring of 1940, Mr. Hitler and his cronies decided to invade Belgium, France, and the Netherlands, putting an end to a false peace and to illusions that some in my country and elsewhere still cherished. Almost overnight, I found myself in a different world. I sold my evening clothes to some of the other girls, got my new diploma, and sought work in the newspaper industry. None of the editors whom I approached for a job were enamored with the idea of a female journalist. But I had made one of the Samuels—one of the last I had encountered in my previous occupation—part of my ambitions. He wrote a letter, praising me, and signed it with his real name and title. And so my life changed radically.

He was the only one of my clients who ever learned my true name, and I his. We both know that we will never share this secret with anyone else.

19

Who sent Inspector Martinengo and his silent partner to interrogate me? Who is responsible for their sudden and unwelcome appearance? Oh, questions, questions! Too many questions. Did they really only show up because my husband is missing? Is that their only excuse, their sole motive? Is it because he has fled and is no longer traceable? Did the London police fail to locate him? And as a result of his disappearance, the Metropolitan sends a telegram to Venice with a simple but, in my case, far-fetching request: to interrogate the missing man's wife. Find out what she knows; find out if she has anything to do with his disappearance. All this seems needlessly exorbitant and plainly a waste of time to me.

Maybe these people assume Michael not only went into hiding but came after me to Venice as well. He may find me here, which means my life might be in danger. He is angry with me (I'm underplaying the whole thing here) and will want to kill me, maybe even in some gruesome way, as a suitable revenge for his perceived suffering. Some people in London are concerned about my safety and about the reputation of his family, and they want to prevent any accidents from occurring. As a result of all those worries, officials, or the police, send these two gentlemen after me. Perhaps from now on I will be shadowed. All for the sake of my safety.

How thoughtful of them.

But why would the police here in Venice pay any attention to me at all, even if pushed by their superiors? I am a stranger, I am an intruder—and even the war no longer offers us British the excuse to hang around here without even the pretext of being a tourist. A new generation of Italians wants no involvement with the former liberators now that the war has ended.

Yet that is exactly what we do—and I mean specifically the British and American secret services, which are particularly interested in certain domestic developments in this country with its strong communist-inspired political activity. Communists who are, furthermore, elected by the people, and as such are considered the dangerous and persistent kind. Some of us come here to spy on the Italians, our so-called allies against the Russians. As a result, my presence is potentially suspicious, since I might be one of those spies.

Communism: the new enemy of all those who call themselves citizens of The Free World. An oppressive and reprehensible ideology, a monstrosity, a disease of the mind. We, the collective West, have recently fought against one totalitarian system, so we will not allow another, equally terrible and just as cruel, to take hold of humanity again. I, for one, do not understand the declarations of love for communism by so many Western intellectuals, their visits to the Soviet Union, or the proliferation of left-wing books and magazines. In Berlin, Paris, and even London, thousands of students march with red banners, quoting Marx, Engels, and Stalin. I do not sympathize with them. They are The Enemy.

But I deviate. A bad habit of mine. Personal discipline must be restored.

Somewhere in London a machine seems to have been set in motion, a machine that extends its tentacles—so to speak—all the way here, to Venice. The conversation with the two police officers has just been concluded, leaving no further consequences, at least for the time being. Inspector Martinengo realized that there was no honor to be gained from further interrogation. I'm here—while events are unfolding in London that the local police might find suspicious. Oh yes, suspicious, no doubt. There is a link between London and my presence here; I will be the first to admit it, but what that link consists of is highly unclear as far as Martinengo is concerned. And I will not enlighten him.

I am going to follow Morse's good advice and not leave Venice for the time being. For now. The departing officers in their cheap civilian clothes have no good advice to give me, no recommendations, and no further questions. At best, they have simply done their duty and will follow up with a brief and meaningless report. Or so I assume.

After this brief break, boredom is threatening to overwhelm me. At the moment, I don't have much to do, and I certainly don't face the intellectual challenges I so desperately crave. So I go looking for some distraction. I find a well-equipped bookstore with English-language books. Several of these are recent: *The Caves of Steel* by Isaac Asimov, *I am Legend* by Richard Matheson, *Messiah* by Gore Vidal, and *The Glass Village* by Ellery Queen. The first two, science fiction and horror, don't interest me much. EQ's detective book can only tempt me for a moment, but I pass it up. Gore Vidal's book seems interesting, so I buy it. Reading an obviously American book here in Venice will make me stand out even more, but *oh well*. Should I care? Living without challenges is so boring. I don't understand how other people do it.

The thing is this: I have to keep sane here in this place. The hotel offers every possible luxury; no complaints there. As such it provides solace for both the soul and the body. The city itself is beautiful in a limited way, but I still have a lot to discover. The bookstore offers a vast selection of books to delve into for months, with new additions likely to arrive on a regular basis.

However, there is another element at play: the lingering uncertainty and tension that lurks just beyond the edge of my perception, ready to strike at any time. Not for a minute am I alone, and yet I am by myself. There are no people around me that I love, and no one to love me. The loneliest place is in a busy crowd, where not a single face has a story to tell me.

On the way back from the bookstore, I stop at a triangular square, sit by a round metal table in a bar, near the window, and open the book. The dust jacket tells me about a new religion aiming to make death attractive, just as it hopes to neutralize the damage caused by all other religions. However, this religion also carries the risk of bringing about a totalitarian society. All religions, after all, tempt or force people to embrace a totalitarian ideology from which escape is impossible.

It is, I suspect, a strange book, and I question my own sanity while reading it. Why did I buy this? I could have chosen something deliciously exciting, something completely nonsensical, any of those other titles. I don't know. I have a hard time analyzing my own motives, as often happens. I usually look for some lame excuse for what I do or have done. I really need to work on that.

I'll return home, I promise myself. I'm going back to London, and everything will be as it should be. Well, it won't be like before, because I definitely don't want to return to that situation. I am not returning to my miserable marriage, and I am certainly not returning to those days when I used expensive hotels for the sins of the flesh and personal gain.

I confess something I don't want to confess. The only time I've been happy was here, in Italy, during the war, during those terrible months, and in the company of violence and death. Only then was I happy. When violence and death rage around you, all other problems cease to exist. That's why people remember so strongly the terrible moments on the battlefield—at war, under fire, in danger. They remember those moments with such force that they are unable to even talk about them with others, especially those who were not there.

There may be a solution to all this: I will return to my old job as a journalist, find myself in a war zone again (there are plenty around in the world), and write about the experience. I'll no doubt find magazines willing to take my product. All this is due to my addiction to risk, while everything else feels like a hazy, nearly intangible, primarily mundane and uninteresting existence.

But first I have to survive Venice.

20

I send a hastily composed telegram to Morse about my meeting with the Italian detectives, the talkative and the silent one. I urge him to contact the British police: it is imperative they find my husband. After all, at some point someone has to appear in court, and I have to be able to extort money from someone. Yes, there is also his family, whom I need to put under just as much pressure. I want to see my miserable years of marriage avenged. This I deserve, in my opinion. My husband is in the dock, publicly humiliated, and forced to admit that he had an affair with another man. It is part of the compensation; it will be part of my purification ritual.

However, there is the risk he will try to avoid all this. The court, on the other hand, might decide to hear this case behind closed doors, given its sensitivity, and so on. And my revenge, that part of my revenge, will therefore be withheld from me. I have already taken this into account. However, if I can prevent this drawback, I will do so.

After sending the telegram, I dress in my leather jacket and tight black trousers and a dark blue angora sweater. Never would Michael want to be seen with me wearing clothes like these. That was the essence of our relationship: I couldn't be who I wanted to be, only the embodiment of his taste, class, and social standing. Nevertheless, with his money, I bought clothes like these on the sly and wore them when he was not around. In London, I went to bars and nightclubs, and no one recognized me. Eventually, however, I became reckless, and he learned of my escapades.

His own escapades turned out to be of a more rigorous nature than my rather innocent dressing up. But maybe we're not all that different in that regard after all. In private, we both embodied another persona than we presented ourselves in public. We both lead double lives. We wore masks and often dressed up to access a world that should not be ours. Well, that should all be in the past, because I'm only living *this* life now. It is a true life, and there is no lie involved anymore. I have money; I have freedom—what more can I ask for?

I know what more I can ask for. You can never have enough money and freedom. The horizon is always farther away and continues to recede. Freedom and wealth are just steps on a long journey, a never-ending one.

I step out of the hotel and walk carelessly along Santa Croce towards the San Simeon Piccolo church, where I admire the dome in the growing dusk. Behind me, I hear the sounds of the train station and the puffing breath of the vaporettos, which are in serious need of replacement.

This city, with its stones, tiles, and steps, as well as its churches and palaces, call out to me: deceiver, liar, poser. What, *me*, who has always served the truth, always has been in the service of that truth? Except for now, for what happened these last weeks, but this is *now*! I could distance myself from these accusations and slander, but for now I have no other place to go. So I lift my chin a little higher and continue walking. I know that the shouting is in my head. It's my imagination speaking.

The darkness is not evenly spread across the city, but where I stand, shadows fold effortlessly over each other. I deeply breathe in the air, fresh but with the taste of wood fires, of newly washed sheets, of old wine as it gushes from a bottle after uncorking. I banish the fear I have of the lagoon's water. I don't want to think about my motives anymore. I just want to be one with the night.

Maybe my plans are futile, and within a year I will find myself in a British cell, despite Morse's good care and creativity. Then Venice, this dark Venice, might prove to have been an illusion, or at most a mere stage in a journey—a very short journey—that took me from London back to London.

At the end of the alley, someone lights a cigarette. I smell the sharp odor of sulfur, followed by smoldering tobacco. A young woman's voice bounces over the water of the nearby canal. Wherever in Venice, you are always near a canal.

On the other side of the alley, the man and the woman are now smoking cigarettes. They exchange a few sentences, like old acquaintances who hardly need words. For the rest, the alley is deserted, between them and me. This part of Venice seems forgotten by history.

21

A young man, dressed in a large, dark overcoat, is leaning against the black iron latticework surrounding the church. He wears a dusty beret, like the one I often see here. His attention is on me. I've heard of young men like him, in places like this, but I don't expect them to be dressed in what appears to be an expensive and elegant, though no longer fashionable, overcoat. Young men like him are common in all major cities, renting out their bodies.

But they must be discreet; there are laws against what they're doing, and the police is always on their heels. Even his once-expensive pre-war overcoat won't save him. His sort lures both men and women into their net. The average citizen despises them because, I assume, of their freedom. They are free from the morality that still prevails in Western countries, especially here in Italy.

However, things may be changing: young people everywhere in Europe are going to influence political choices because the postwar generation has become eligible to vote. It will depend on the youth whether there will be more individual freedom in times to come and whether the suffocating cloak of religion, civility, and morality will be thrown off. Revealing what, and being superseded by what, I don't know. Anyway, the revolution will happen, one way or another, in whatever form. I hope to be part of it, or at least a privileged bystander.

But let's focus our attention on this particular young man and the potential danger his presence entails. The danger lies in the cliché: a desperate foreign woman on her way to middle age falls for the deceptively boyish charms of a well-dressed gigolo. That's what this story is all about. I have every intention of avoiding the cliché, and I'm not desperate either. If I make the wrong decision, it will be out of boredom. At least then I will be spending the remainder of my time here in Venice in a most pleasant way, a succession of nights in my luxurious room with a warm body next to me. I believe I am entitled to such pleasure. I'm still young, after all, and life hasn't always given me much in the way of affection and love.

I face a specific risk however, a distinct type of peril, in which a shameful incident in Venice could become widely known back home, potentially jeopardizing my prospects in a British court. After all, I'm still married; I can't afford infidelity. I also rely on the hotel's lack of surveillance, and my success in hiding my unwanted visitor and the physical results of our nightly escapades.

However, I weigh this risk against . . . against what? Against the pleasure I can expect from this young man? Is this where we are going—me and this young lad, who may have no plans at all for a rich foreign tourist, a lonely one at that?

He's clearly on to something, this young man, because he slowly advances towards me, calm, almost seductive. He knows he doesn't have to rush. He is confident that the foreign visitor won't flee. He knows she is a potential customer, precisely because of her eccentric clothing; a target, or prey, whatever. That's me, the prey. He knows this because I keep looking at him without attention or consideration for my surroundings. I don't care what people think of me, my intentions, or my reason for being at this place.

"Bona sera, Signora," he says politely, sonorously, as calmly as the rest of his demeanor. He knows how little effort he has to make to seduce me. Based on his experience, I will fall into his trap without further ado. "Non parlo inglese o tedesco." With an apologetic and disarming smile.

So he suspects that I'm British or German, which, given my blond hair and figure, isn't a bad guess.

Our conversation will be limited, I'm afraid, but that's the premise we both accept. And under these circumstances, there will be no need for much conversation, although I would like to learn more about him. I know a few standard Italian phrases, a vocabulary of a hundred words or so, and I make do with that.

I ask him, "Ho fame, andiamo a cena?"

He smiles. "La gastronomia Italiana è fra le migliori," he says. Which he assumes I will understand. And agree with.

And with that, with that worthless, tourist-attracting phrase, the ice is broken, as they say. It will be clear to him that I barely speak Italian, apart from what I learned during the war. His name is Antonio, he tells me with a smile. "Tony," he adds. I shake my head. "Antonio," I say. He's not American. Let's not talk about the Americans. And I would like to explore Italian gastronomy with him.

22

Despite our almost non-existent communication, we spend a pleasant hour in a small trattoria where apparently no tourists venture, only Venetians. He has chosen a place where nobody seems to know him. I understand his prudence: he wants to conceal the nature of his activities, to wit picking up and seducing foreign tourists, and so he avoids being seen by acquaintances. He will not take me to the neighborhood where he lives. Even here, his gaze is only occasionally on me while he carefully scrutinizes our surroundings.

I have a fair idea of the state of public and private morals in this city, and I am aware of its historic reputation for sin and all sorts of social transgressions. I have, however, never experienced this reputation firsthand, and have plucked it from historic and literary sources. As do most of the tourists, I'm sure. Antonio, on the other hand, is just being careful, and intends on avoiding problems with the law. Anyway, if we should be accosted by police, I will feign total ignorance and innocence, and why can't I have a drink with a local young man in a bar? Surely, officer, there is no law against consorting with the locals? But this ignorant victim will be fully aware of the irony of the situation, specifically in my case. I never was a victim, never ignorant.

Antonio has not only ordered drinks but some snacks as well, from which he eats a few morsels. The wine is excellent, but he hardly touches it. We manage a whole bottle, however, which is to say, I drink most of it, albeit at a leisurely pace. I am aware of his game: he wants me in the right frame of mind for whatever is coming and will not want me to back down on what for him will prove to be a profitable deal. I settle the check while remaining relatively sober.

Then, standing outside in a chilly breeze, he takes my hand in a gentle but firm grip and whispers an amount in dollars, not lira. I confess that I have no dollars with me, but I do have British pounds. He mentions the same amount, which is significantly advantageous given the difference in exchange rates between the two currencies. It is not a large sum, and I can afford it.

My hotel? I'd rather not, I say, because I can't get him past reception, and I don't want him in my room either. All right, he admits he has something else to offer, and a little later we walk down a labyrinth of alleys where I quickly lose all sense of direction. So far in this story, I've been trying to avoid the cliché while maintaining my dignity, but it now appears that I'm failing in both areas.

I tend to forgive myself for that failure.

We arrive at a small square, where some young people hang out, smoking Italian cigarettes and leaning against rusting pre-war bicycles. One wears a red beret, the other a worn leather jacket. They cast a few glances our way, yet their interest remains minimal. Antonio is my safe conduct. I realize that these young people were still children during the war, and that this experience will have scarred them for life. The same goes for Antonio. If I spoke his language better, I would ask him about these experiences, but I'm not going to. And maybe I don't want it, either.

I know all too well how the war wreaked havoc on this country and its people.

He takes me to what appears to be a guest house, but there is no doorman or anyone controlling access. The building is dilapidated, a feature I've grown accustomed to in this area. He leads me up a narrow wooden staircase that remains unpainted after a century or so. As are the walls and doors. The whole exudes careless poverty, although the entire building is free of foul odors or suggestive sounds. The room we enter contains some simple furniture and is neat, without luxury or frills.

He quickly closes the curtain on the only window, and lights a hissing gas lamp that gives off a somewhat comforting golden glow. If this is his room, his mother raised him well, instilling in him a sense of order and cleanliness. However, it's likely that she won't be aware of his journey to this profession. I suspect his parents are dead. In this unhappy land, death has mowed away entire generations.

At first, I am hesitant to accept his soft hands, as they seem to want to strip me of my clothes. They look like a girl's hands, feverish yet careful. He understands my hesitation. It turns out that he is very empathetic. Behind a screen is a small chest of drawers, a bowl, an earthen carafe with clear water, soap in another small bowl, and some surprisingly soft towels. This room is used often and probably for the same purpose. He leaves for a moment, and I quickly wash myself, without shame, without hesitation. Then I crawl in the bed, naked. He comes back, sees me in the bed, smiles, says something I don't understand, quickly takes off his clothes, and slides next to me.

I lose all concept of time.

His hands, those non-masculine hands, possess a magic that I have never experienced before, with no man, and certainly not with my husband.

Definitely not with my husband.

For a moment, I am less lonely. Why has life withheld this balm from me for such a long time? Why hasn't life treated me more nicely? I don't wait for an answer, but enjoy the moments.

I come twice, way too loudly, which he finds amusing.

I desire nothing more than this harmony, and that warm body next to me in bed. But I can't stay all night.

Why not?

I don't know.

I only realize it's one in the morning when I check my watch. He put out the gas lamp; I don't remember when. He doesn't sleep. I explain, in a few words of Italian, that I have to leave. This puts an end to our intimacy. I discreetly leave the money on a chair as an offering to this god of fertility. After dressing, I exit the building. His scent still clings to me. I will lose myself in this maze of passages and alleys. It takes a while, but then I find the hotel. At the reception, no one looks up at me.

My own room is dark, cold, and strange. I am all alone again, a situation not entirely unwelcome. Not at this time. I want to sleep. My arms and legs feel sluggish, almost useless. I turn on a table lamp. At first I don't notice anything, but then a strange feeling creeps up on me. Something has changed in the room. She is subtly different from when I left it earlier.

I realize what it is.

Someone has searched my room. Opened the drawers, examined the closets, inspected my stuff, looked at the tags on all the clothes, searched for something, for evidence of my fornication, of my lies, looking for the real reason I'm here.

Discreetly, so I wouldn't notice.

I notice it anyway. I just *know*.

Someone was bold enough to break into this hotel room, and look for something here, all while keeping in mind that nothing should make me suspect this intrusion. That did not work. I know for sure. And I also know what the intruder was looking for. He didn't find it because it's safely in a bank vault.

The intruder will be disappointed. He will probably make a new attempt to get his hands on that diary later. He may employ alternative methods, potentially involving brutality and violence. I have to arm myself against him and his kind. I have to take action. But how do I do that? It is difficult for me to take this to the police because I do not want to inform them about the diary.

23

It is inevitable, an inevitable intermezzo in this story, but we once more have to return to that other Italy, during the warm, humid summer of the fatal year 1944. Fatal for fascism, in any case. Fatal for the most backward ideology on the planet—although communism later turned out to be no better, and responsible for even more victims.

Soon after my arrival in the war zone, I had little left of the charms I used in London to get this assignment. I was unwashed, dusty, dirty, and smelled no different than the soldiers around me. I only wanted one thing: to help defeat the fascists. And write about the collective effort.

It was absolutely unheard of for a civilian, and a woman at that, to march with troops in a war zone. But no one asked me about my motives or credentials, and I wasn't going to question such an effortless acceptance. I was, after all, a war correspondent. The letters of introduction, written by the right people to the right people, did their job well. I even had the honor of becoming the mascot for a particular army unit. And I have experienced the worst of battle.

The worst? The entire campaign in Italy was incredibly brutal and deadly. Corpses uncounted, suffering immeasurable. I was there when, in May 1944, British and Canadian troops advanced from Pignatoro—just north of the Liri River—to Ceprano, breaking through the German Gustav Line. The terrain was hardly suitable for the heavy equipment the Allies brought with them, which they later would need in the plains towards Rome. Some specialized mountain troops had suitable artillery that could be transported in parts with the aid of pack animals or jeeps, but these troops were not always available. Entire columns of tanks and trucks advanced slowly over the few passable roads, past the few bridges that had not been sabotaged, or the Bailey bridges hastily built by army engineers. Occasionally, German artillery from higher positions would shell troops, causing the war to stall for a day or two. The only advantage for the Allied forces was their air superiority. But in mountainous areas, this is usually not of much use to infantrymen.

We heard what things were like elsewhere. In particular, we heard about the Goumiers, irregular soldiers from the Berber tribes of the Moroccan Atlas Mountains, who had joined the Free French forces. They wore French army uniforms, but also their gold earrings, striped coats, and sometimes a necklace made of the ears of killed German and Italian soldiers. They received hardly any pay but made up with plunder and rape, with the army leadership turning a blind eye because otherwise these soldiers would simply go home again. However, thousands of Italians, including women, children, men, and the elderly, fell victim to the misdeeds of those Goumiers, succumbing to rape and violence. Stories circulated of young girls who had been raped by six or seven of those men, young women who were abused and left with deep wounds (physical and psychological). Some went crazy, others committed suicide. Nothing was done about it, because they were only powerless Italians from the countryside.

The British and Canadian soldiers who heard these stories were disgusted by such barbaric behavior. They admitted to having used violence themselves, including against civilians, and there had been rapes (rarely punished), but not on this scale and not with this degree of ferocity. As if that made any difference. As if it makes any difference to the victims whether you are raped, tortured, or killed by enemies or by friendly troops.

But this was not a subject I could write about. My editors expected stories of heroic deeds, glory, and victory over the German monster. Stories of pitiful casualties on our side and raped women did not fit into the political rhetoric of the allied nations.

Soon after, I would take the life of an enemy, contributing to the ultimate triumph over fascism. War, at least on the ground, is usually a matter for young people, and they are its most prominent victims. More recently, I visited one of those cemeteries in Normandy, where the bodies of fallen American and British soldiers lie—those who died during the landings in June 1944 and the following days. Boys aged eighteen, nineteen, and twenty. Children, almost. Not only the dead, but also the living—those who emerged damaged from the war—were young and vulnerable. For them, the living, those returning to their country, their city, their family—everything had changed. Experience has taught me that even those who escaped death had forfeited a portion of their humanity.

After the war, I encountered soldiers. Soldiers who had close encounters with Death. They didn't view Death as their master, but rather as their slave, one who repeatedly rebelled and had a tendency to serve the enemy. None of them talked much about their experiences. They did not talk with their family, spouse, children, or parents. They couldn't share experiences with anyone except those who had been there and had seen what they had seen. What they had seen was humanity's moral vacuum.

This is war—the absolute moral vacuum of humanity. In this realm, the absence of other emotions necessitates the use of pain. And they take that pain home with them—those soldiers who survive. That's all they bring. They leave the rest behind: hope, pity, even fear. Suicide is more common among those returning from the battlefield than among the rest of the population. More attention is gradually being paid to the problem, but too little and—for many—too late.

24

Morning. This morning is unlike any other, yet it evokes the same doubtful feeling I often experience at this time of day. Quite a few of my memories are linked to this early, dim light: a neglected house, the overpowering smell of coal stoves, of cooked vegetables, of unwashed clothes, the voices of neighbors through the thin walls, the girls at school who had no ambitions except to work in a shop or factory, and the boring lessons about the English kings and the colonies and God. If our childhood shapes our future lives, then I faced certain doom from an early age. But I escaped my fate. And I did all that by myself, and there was nothing heroic about it.

Perhaps it was less a process of escape than of survival. I survived my childhood. Alternatively, none of us, not a single individual, emerges from this existence untouched.

Mornings are the moment when you cut the umbilical cord with the night and with oblivion.

I awaken, rise, and open the curtains, revealing a cloudy, gray light and a similarly gray Venice, seemingly constructed from sharp-angled pieces of basalt and red brick—magnificent, indeed, but not at this hour. I then survey the room. She is as before, and yet she is not. Nothing is the same as before. The river of time flows irresistibly through our body, through our existence. We will never be who we were before. We will never be the same again. A universe without Time is unthinkable. But thanks to time, we can change, we can become someone different from who we were before.

I have read Proust, as well as his inspiration, Bergson.

And so, sometime over the past few years, I have come to this conclusion: man's problem is that he is never satisfied with his limitations, because there is a huge universe out there, an immense challenge for us, a universe with many unanswered questions. Our consciousness has enforced this unfortunate side effect on us: our limitless and unquenchable curiosity. We want to know everything, and we certainly want to know it right now.

At the same time, we are intellectually unable to comprehend everything or solve all mysteries because we are limited in space and time. This frustrates us to no end, and so many give up trying. Most people are not even interested in pursuing larger goals in life. They settle for common things and simple forms of entertainment. They engage in sports, listen to popular music, frequent bars, and simply bide their time, not really applying themselves to anything. They refuse to do any deep thinking and deny its value. The mysteries of the universe and time are of no interest to them, even irrelevant. As such, the world is in danger of sliding into suffocating superficiality.

Morning, then. It's another day in this perplexing and largely indifferent city. A city that somehow seems to lie outside of space and time, as if moored on a wrong and, to us, mysterious shore of history. It won't be long before I start to believe in her many myths and legends. Specifically those about demons at the bottom of the lagoon, only to surface during the darkest nights of December, close to New Year's Eve, and to swallow up fearless but foolish gondoliers and their passengers.

I have two unresolved issues this morning: the diary and my divorce. The first problem is simple enough to solve. I forget the safe, which will not be opened until half a century from now, or when the rent is no longer paid. At that point, what happens to the diary is not my problem and will eventually become irrelevant.

The financial arrangements associated with my second problem are of a more pressing nature. Morse is dealing with it, and my future lies in his capable hands. But in that telegram of his, I heard him hesitate. I saw his slightly uncertain words. I could see that he was not entirely convinced of a favorable outcome for my case. There is too much that can go wrong.

And what if the lawsuit does indeed go wrong? What happens when a judge rejects my claims as irrelevant? My soon-to-be former husband may not award me a penny in the divorce. In that case, we will divorce without assigning him any blame, and he will not face any financial consequences. His family, on the other hand, will still be willing to give me hush money. So anyway, I will have some sort of financial security, but I still want more of it.

I don't expect to see Antonio again, with his soft hands, brooding look, and saffron voice. But at breakfast he turns up at the buffet, which he replenishes with sandwiches and cakes in a calm, professional manner, dressed like all the other waiters. It is indeed him, my Venetian gigolo, whom I left in his bed early this morning, still dozing and only semi-conscious. Now he is here, in this hotel, in a neat uniform (black slacks, white shirt, dark gray sleeveless vest), elegant and clearly trained in this craft. He is not looking in my direction; it's possible that he doesn't know I'm here, as he appears unaware of anything. I didn't tell him I'm staying at this hotel.

A short while later, as he passes by once more, his gaze sweeps over me, revealing that he is familiar with my identity, and my presence does not astonish him. One thing is immediately clear: he knows all about me. This past night, and the meeting that preceded it, none of it was a coincidence. He had seen me earlier in the hotel, followed me, waited for me, and knew he would leave a lasting impression. There is no coincidence involved. Everything is part of a plan, and it is undoubtedly well thought out. Only I am not aware of the existence of this plan or of its extent.

And if this turns out to be a trap, then I fell into it willingly and with open eyes.

He now disappears back into the kitchen, and it takes a while before he reappears. His job seems to consist of replenishing the buffet. Other waiters take orders for coffee or tea and bring the requested drink to the guests' tables; he doesn't. There is a division of labor, perhaps based on language knowledge. He cannot converse with the guests, so his role here is limited.

Calm down. All of this may seem strange, but it does not necessarily imply a conspiracy in which I am the unwilling target of a gang or a criminal organization. All this is perhaps limited to Antonio, his attentiveness to certain types of customers (lonely women of a certain age—that would be me), and his interest in making a profit from those women's loneliness. Maybe this is all there is to it. If possible, he will wait for me again after his service, at the same gate, with the same intention. Or not. There are undoubtedly other lonely women of a certain age residing in the hotel. They are not safe from him either.

Do I have room in my life for him and his plans? Actually not; no, I don't. Therefore, I should avoid him from now on. I must avoid any form of temptation, because behind a pillar or a tree or a shrub a private detective may be watching me, someone sent by my in-laws, with the aim of catching me in any indiscretion that could undermine my claims to a share of their fortune. No walk through the city will remain unnoticed, and I fear that my meeting with Antonio last night may have already led to my doom. A report about it has been written. The family has been duly informed. They are already reflecting on this matter this same morning, and the knives are being sharpened. They will be considering a strategy whose sole and unique goal is to discredit me in front of the press, the public, and the judiciary. Then, I will lose all my financial gains.

Done business. If a private detective observes me, photographs me, and if he did so last night, there is nothing I can do about it anymore. I may have to inform Morse so he can formulate an appropriate strategy leading to some sort of exit. Whatever that is. A strategy, perhaps, that neutralizes those of my opponents, as far as this would be possible. How he manages, is his business. Any claim made by a private detective may perhaps, if I'm lucky, prove to have little weight in a British court. Public opinion has no further say in my fate because it lies in the hands of that same court. It is a matter of awarding damages; there is nothing more to it. There is no actual crime involved, at least not on my part.

My husband's absence is an advantage in this respect: he cannot defend himself until he shows up again.

I feel a little reassured again. Let a private detective follow me. A walk with an attractive young man on the streets of Venice is not an offense, even if I disappeared in his company into an obscure house, only to reappear the next morning. At worst, this is what will be read in the detective's report, but nothing more. As I said, such a report does not have to carry much weight in a court because magistrates and judges might not like private detectives.

Antonio casually takes one last look at me. That look holds a promise, which I alone register. I hope so anyway.

25

I cannot consult my agenda because I do not have it with me. There is no calendar anywhere in the hotel, nor is there a public clock. The management clearly does not want guests to feel forced by the passage of time. Nothing should put pressure on them. The hotel is a place out of time, just like this city, where the dead conspire with future generations. This place exists, but it has no connection to the rest of civilization. This makes communicating and doing business with others difficult.

However, I seem unable to escape the obligations of this society, as a hurried messenger finds me in the drawing room and hands me a telegram from Morse. Tomorrow, the trial will begin in my case against my husband and his family. So far, the court has not requested my presence. My written statement seems to suffice, for the time being.

When I tried to find my way into the society of extremely wealthy men who, for all kinds of reasons, stayed at hotels like The Ritz or used the bar a decade and a half ago, I was barely prepared for the lack of sophistication of my future customers. *Customers*. It's a word I never used at the time. A shopkeeper has customers, just as a plumber or a tailor does. I had friends or protectors. I was not the only girl in those circles, nor the only one acting on her own initiative. I didn't understand the term at the time, but I didn't have a pimp to defend me or advocate for my (and particularly his) interests. I learned to be independent of anyone, especially men. We had arrangements and understandings—but I was never their property. And I never will be. Search for my ultimate motive, and there you are.

That fog- and fear-ridden era on the eve of war was characterized by nervous agitation among the upper classes, as well as their inability to properly face the painful and often threatening truths associated with Germany and fascism. But the period (actually the end of a period) also came with an urge to loosen all inhibitions, as long as this happened in private. A well-intentioned young lady like myself, with a solid education, well-read, and cultured, although from a relatively modest background, but without any reservations or embarrassment, could earn a nice penny back then. I nearly always ended up in the bed of some semi-prominent or wealthy man, most of whom were already past the age where sexual acts were their main motivation. In many cases, I used only my mouth and hands to entertain the generous benefactor in the safety of his own room, usually after a lavish meal and much alcoholic consumption on his part. For some of them, however, I was a public companion, nothing more. They needed me as a status symbol, someone who was both beautiful and intelligent, capable of engaging in a variety of conversations without delving into politics. Presentable at any social occasion, at least those where wives were not supposed to be present. Sometimes I was a niece or a friend's daughter. Payment for my services was always generous, even when I had only provided an evening of pleasant company without sexual acts afterwards.

I wonder if similar activities are also held in this hotel here in Venice. In that regard, I safely assume that times will probably not have changed. The rich still have the power to enslave others, erasing their prey's personality and future. There will always be masters and slaves. I was once a slave; now I have the intention to be a master. What I once used to be, young Antonio was to me last night. I am well aware of the irony of this situation.

I am now shamelessly tempted by vulgar touristic urges: I visit the somewhat charming Piazza di San Marco and manage to drink a cappuccino on the busy terrace of Café Florian while I try to read an Italian newspaper, in order not to stand out too much. Florian has the honor of being the very first coffee house in Europe to open its doors in 1683. Further on, there is the equally attractive and expensive Quadri terrace, which is currently its main competitor on the Piazza.

The tourists marvel at the square, especially the Campanile. Most likely, they are unaware that the building is not original. Its construction was begun in 888 and took some six centuries to be fully completed in 1514. The destruction occurred at a slightly faster pace: in 1902, it abruptly collapsed and underwent subsequent rebuilding to its original specifications. The basilica houses the remains of Saint Marc the Evangelist. In 828, they were smuggled from his grave in Alexandria across Moorish territory in a basket labeled *pork* and received a hero's welcome in Venice. A dead hero, admittedly. For the cynic, it is unlikely that these were the true remains of the saint. Anyway, that didn't spoil the fun at the time.

I have visited many cities, but even in London, the past is not as pertinently present as here. The history of buildings, streets, and squares goes back much further than anything to be found in the English capital. And many famous names were guests here, passing through the city on their way to somewhere else, or sharing a significant part of their lives with its walls. André Gide, Marco Polo, Casanova, Friedrich Nietzsche, and Donatien de Sade walked on the same tiles as I do, and what they ate was probably not much different from what I eat here. Louis Aragon tried to commit suicide in a hotel in 1928, after having burned the manuscript of *La Défense de l'Infini*, all fifteen hundred pages of it, a year earlier in Madrid. His (almost successful) physical suicide appropriately echoes his literary one—a noble attempt to provide a literary career with a fitting end.

Not entirely unexpectedly, Van Rijn reappears. Our previous conversation went nowhere, but he persists. I'm still here, and he probably suspects that I didn't sell the diary to another party. He sits down at my table in the restaurant, something which I deem extremely rude. I realize that my hotel admits just anyone. There seems to be no security worth mentioning. No wonder rooms are not safe. I wonder if he was the one who searched mine. Who else?

"Twenty thousand," he says. He doesn't even blink, not even on account of such a substantial figure.

The amount is becoming increasingly generous, that much is certain. The transaction is therefore all the more suspicious, the fate of the diary doomed. As an enemy of fascism, I cannot let that happen. People I don't know feel threatened by it. I want to maintain that threat because I am emotionally and morally the enemy of these people. But of course I run into danger if I persist in my stubbornness.

"It's not for sale," I say.

"Everything is for sale," he says. He makes it sound easy.

I am aware of the truth behind his words. Everything and everyone is for sale. Even I was once for sale. Or at least for rent.

"Dangerous enemies," he warns me. "You are making yourself dangerous enemies, something you can't afford."

"War," I say. "I have some experience with war. I was shot at by dangerous enemies. And I survived."

"That wasn't personal."

"This is?"

He sighs at my persistence. "Not as such. But on the other hand, maybe it is. You are the accidental owner of an object that some consider valuable. You have no reason to want to keep it, at least not at this price. Perhaps your stubbornness is morally or ethically motivated. That is a dangerous situation, although it is certainly to your credit. And even my superiors respect you for it. You have personally experienced the war, which presents its own set of challenges. Moral and ethical positions have little chance of survival during a war. You know that, and I know it too."

"There's peace now." But I would have to contradict his statement. Morals and ethics must be preserved and strengthened precisely because of the war. Otherwise, what hope does humanity have?

"Peace?" he says indignantly. "Only people in your privileged position can be forgiven for making such stupid assumption. Some wars never end. They never do."

"Which wars do you mean?"

"Ideological wars. Those between systems of thought. Those between cultures, in the social sense of the word. Capitalism versus communism, to name the main one. Religions, too. West versus east. It's merely a never-ending retelling of the same old tale. Those things, those contradictions, have been around for centuries. These are old wars, which sometimes flare up into real, violent conflicts."

"So the diary," I say, "is a weapon."

"Of course it is. Everything written down—the written word in any form—can and will be a weapon. People continue to place significant value on written words. Propaganda is a military strategy; words are bullets. And in the end, the lie always turns out to cause more harm than the truth can heal. That is something we both learned, didn't we?"

"It is a weapon because this diary mentions names your clients want to keep hidden and which were not mentioned in Nuremberg. Of people who escaped their fate."

"That is correct," he admits. "I have no difficulty confirming your statement. That is why the amount offered is so high. This is a conscious strategy on our part. You are not a moral person, Mrs. Barth. You are not. I am aware of your affairs in England. Your morality is very selective. There is no reason for you to refuse my offer any longer. Especially when there are certain alternatives, unfriendly alternatives . . ."

"You are threatening me; that's what it comes down to." He also insults me, but I'll overlook that for the time being. I can take my revenge on him later. If the opportunity ever arises.

"Indeed. You may see this as a threat."

He's just a little too honest for my liking. But this leaves nothing to be desired in terms of clarity. "Your clients," I say, "are therefore willing to do anything for the manuscript."

"That's right. Literally everything."

"Their problem is that they don't know where it is."

"No, they don't. You know where it is, though. And extracting information from people, well, that is an activity my clients are experts in." He pauses and continues to stare at me. But nothing happens anymore. He understands this conversation is once again going nowhere and gets up. "Think about it. I mean it. Your situation is precarious. Very precarious. No one here will protect you."

And with those words, he leaves the restaurant.

I get up and follow him. He doesn't notice and leaves the hotel. I follow him outside. He has already reached the other side of the street. He stops there, but he doesn't notice me because he is engaged in conversation with another man.

I know that other man.

It's my love for one night, Antonio.

26

The plot now becomes complex. Or maybe it doesn't. Maybe the situation is very clear and obvious now, but I don't see it. I don't see where the labyrinth exits are located. I don't see the writing on the wall, so to speak. I make enemies, that much is certain, and I'm making them here in Venice, which I can't afford. The solution is obvious: outdo my enemies. This will have to be my strategy, without delay.

What do I care about Rosenberg's diary? Why do I let history weigh me down so much? Van Rijn is right: I am not a moral person, at least not anymore. While fighting for control of my in-laws' money, I denied my moral soul, without being able to admit it. However, because of that denial, the diary should mean nothing to me.

However, I see myself as a complex person. And I know I am stubborn. My understanding of the truth is changing, and it's not a positive development. I have become prone to lies and deceit. I am embroiled in a struggle to get my hands on money that is not my own, although I feel entitled to it. On the other side, I'm refusing a bundle of cash for a manuscript I consider of no importance. I need to navigate in between these extremes, these contradictions.

Both cases have one thing in common. My in-laws are part of my enemies' camp. The same holds true for the unidentified individuals seeking to purchase Rosenberg's journal. Both wear, as far as I'm concerned, the mask of fascism, of self-righteous capitalism bourgeoisie. I'm including the men at the Ritz, the men who shot at me in Italy, and all those who murdered millions for the sake of an ideology. The men now seek to safeguard their interests by destroying a diary that bears their names. They're all the same men. They resemble my spouse and his relatives.

My motive can be found there. There is a reason for my stubborn behavior.

27

Antonio and Van Rijn. It is impossible to imagine them as conspirators, linked in the same plot, as different as I imagine them to be. Their portrayal as a pair of crooks seems excessively satirical. Despite this, the plot does make sense. In this city, even coincidence is suspect. Indeed, I am under constant attack and threat from all directions. That's certainly how it feels. I urgently need to seize the initiative and keep it.

But how do I manage? There is one option: leave here immediately. I suspect that my opponent, Van Rijn, will not want to follow me all the way to London. On the other hand, why wouldn't he? Certainly his employers might have the funds to send him after me.

I don't know the extent of the plot against me. I'm completely in the dark; that's my main problem. Involving the police is of course out of the question, primarily because I know nothing about Edvardo's fate, and I might even not want to trust the police. When I saw Edvardo that last time, he didn't seem to be doing so well. I believe he has passed away by now, but it's unlikely that anyone will find his body. If they find it, the police will likely search for a murderer, adding me to their list of primary suspects, and perhaps someone will recall him from the hotel. This is my problem: the wrong people remember the wrong things, and the police draw the wrong conclusions.

As far as I'm concerned, Edvardo not showing up—either dead or alive—is a good thing. I will applaud his non-existence. If he makes an appearance again, things might get complicated—for me in the first place. Of course, it's entirely my fault—on account of my own stubbornness. I should have given him the money for the diary and then thrown the bloody thing in the lagoon, in a bag weighted down with stones. I should have then returned to London. Forget that stupid battle against fascism and the rest of the world. Not my battle.

But I could not. I could not do any of that. However, none of this currently resolves my dilemma. I still don't want the diary to fall in the hands of the wrong people, and I want to get out of here alive.

I continue to observe Van Rijn and Antonio for a moment, but I don't gain any insight. Their conversation is brief and apparently emotionless. They exchange information. This is enough for me. I know now that I can't trust Antonio. He will no longer lure me into his bed.

Unless.

Maybe I should inverse the current situation and take matters in hand myself. I could try to find out who this Van Rijn fellow is and whom he works for. I need to know how much of a threat he and his employers pose, as well as why I must fear them. Who are these people?

When both gentlemen take leave and Antonio disappears to the left, I start to follow Van Rijn. He seems to know every-thing about me, and I am going to inverse the roles. This will ultimately turn into a classic spy story set in a chilly Venice. I've seen a couple of crime movies and know how to behave while shadowing someone in the streets. And there's the tricks I learned during the war. All of this is now useful.

I continue to follow Van Rijn, but on the other side of the street, and I leave enough space between us not to be too obvious. I assume he doesn't expect to be followed, certainly not by me. This is, of course, his main mistake: he only sees me as his almost powerless, although very stubborn, victim. In the end, I will do exactly what the conspirators wish, or so they presume. Well, they are presuming wrong, and I am going to prove that.

Following Van Rijn, I enter the Venice of the narrow, cobblestoned alleys and the small, winding passerelles, the amateurishly plastered blank walls with their high windows, the dark, low-ceilinged shops where no tourists come, the noisy ateliers, the butchers and bakers that have not changed their trade nor the interior of their shops in decades, and the crumbling boarding houses for listless and restless souls. No guide can serve me better than the man I secretly follow. I am now an accomplished member of his conspiracy: I shadow a man on Venice's streets. Never thought it would come to this.

The city always confuses and surprises this unsuspecting visitor. I remember its main sights—the festive but mysterious masks in the shops, the handcrafted leather goods, and the eateries with heady red wine in large bottles. Local residents behave carelessly, at worst haughtily, but they are like all Italians: if you speak a few words of their language, you are their guest, almost their friend. They understand their own culture like no one else does, and they like to brag about it, but they don't have much patience with religion. In the countryside, priests used to rule the roost, but not because people were deeply religious. It was, in fact, a tradition of resignation that allowed their power to exist. In cities, things are and have been different: public order is an elusive ambiguity, with magistracy, elected politicians, and populists wielding uncontrolled power and sharing their often sharp opinions in the newspapers and weekly magazines. Everyone belongs to at least one network, none of which has anything to do with the much-hated government. Neither of these networks is connected to the Church, which only plays a symbolic role in Venice.

We end up at the shady Campo San Solo. Casanova was a guest in an adjacent palazzo, the Ca' Soranzo. He was adopted by an ailing senator and eventually even ennobled. There is not a single building in this city that does not testify to the passage of some historical figure. They often broke down doors, got drunk, chased women, and sometimes raped minors at will, even children. Everything was possible in those days, at least if you were rich. In fact, the same freedom still applies. As long as you're rich.

Behind the square lie a number of bridges, and further on there will be the Grand Canal, but Van Rijn stops on the square itself, at the southern end, under some skeletal trees. Housewives wrapped tightly in layers of clothing eye him suspiciously and send the children indoors. He takes a black woolen cap from the pocket of his overcoat and puts it on. This makes him less noticeable. He stands there for some time, smoking a cigarette. I hide beneath a colonnade, attempting to remain unnoticed. To my right are stone columns displaying wealthy families' emblems. Most tiles on the square are cracked and need to be replaced, which will not happen. A city such as this takes pride in its physical decay, until the living conditions become dangerous.

Then Van Rijn suddenly has company. A woman, dark-haired, tall, and slim. Handsome too, with the regular, almost sculpted features of ancient nobility. Under her gray fur coat, she wears brown leather boots with sturdy heels. I have the impression she is otherwise naked, but that is a private fantasy. She asks the questions, and then seems to comment on the three or four words he answers. This is not an amorous relationship; he seems much too nervous. The way he puffs on his cigarette and finally throws it away reveals his restlessness, his displeasure. Something's going on between them, and it is not something he enjoys. Things don't go as he expected. Of course they don't: this woman expects him to bring the famous diary. Now he's standing here empty-handed, and she's not happy. Not at all.

I'm glad he's having a challenging time and has to admit his failure. If our paths cross again, I will be equipped with a few strategies and a unique understanding of his position. Cards that I will be able to play if things go right for me. On the other hand, I have to take into account the complexity of the plot. There are several people involved who may not show as much patience as he does, at least not with me. I should definitely exercise more caution in this situation. The woman looks ferocious; she does. I'd like to keep my distance from her.

She ends the conversation with a short gesture of disdain. Van Rijn slinks away, beaten dog, unfaithful and failed servant that he is.

I don't follow him. He no longer interests me. I'm keeping an eye on her. She spends some time in the square, seemingly indecisive and needing to consider her options. She doesn't exactly look like the kind of woman who suffers from indecisiveness, but like someone who can make tough decisions when necessary. And who has no patience with half-hearted people like Van Rijn. Maybe he'll disappear from the scenery now. I certainly don't notice him anymore. Someone else, either a woman or another accomplice, will take his place. Someone will act with greater decisiveness, striving to achieve tangible outcomes quickly. Someone who will have no patience with me. I consider myself warned.

And so I follow her. She now walks south, crosses the Grand Canal, and a little later we reach the Campo San Angelo, where she enters an ordinary house, passing a door to the side of a tobacco and spirits shop. Above the shop are three floors, each with three windows. Flats, I assume. I assume she resides here, or this is the central location of the conspiracy, which aims to preserve the legacy of the Thousand Year Reich. I take shelter again, on the other side of the Campo, and keep an eye on the building.

28

Unfortunately, night swiftly falls like a theater curtain at the end of the performance, and almost with the same alarming rapidity, and my position as an observer becomes useless and equally untenable. I don't enjoy playing this role—that of spy, secret agent, and potential victim in a sordid plot orchestrated by dark and sinister figures. I should be concerned with other things: with the inheritance of my inheritance, with the lawsuit against my former lover, with protecting my future financial affairs. I cannot entrust everything to Morse, even though he receives sufficient compensation to ensure my safety and stability in London, amidst the potential storms that may arise in the near future.

I'm wasting my time here with that stupid diary, which I didn't even buy, but which was pressed upon me. I have no obligation to Edvardo (wherever he may be), but I want to keep to the moral high ground if I can.

However, I remain ever doubtful, constantly considering how to keep my morality in check, and equally afraid of making mistakes that could potentially damn my soul. I made mistakes in the past. In the grander scheme of things, I want to set the record straight. There is no God, I'm sure, and no soul either, but I need to be able to live with my forever doubting self.

133

While night falls, nothing happens. The woman seems to enjoy her stay in the flat and has not shown herself at a window, so her exact location is unknown to me. Lights are on on each of the three floors above the store, but the curtains are closed. I have no idea where she is or what she's up to. After her, no one else entered the building. I'm clearly wasting my time.

Because of how hungry I am, I return to the hotel and its restaurant. At least there's nothing wrong with my appetite. I am tempted to have a bottle of wine, although I need to curb my alcohol consumption, or I will become a pale, fat middle-aged woman by my mid-forties. I then will need to pay for erotic pleasures with the likes of Antonio. That treacherous Antonio, who was nevertheless good in bed.

Yes, he was devilishly good in bed.

Better than my husband ever was—the conceited, ostentatious, overweight bourgeois who never climaxed with me no matter what I tried. Who never wanted to give me any pleasure either. And now I know why: because he wasn't interested in me at all, only in young men. Young men like my Antonio. In a sense, I am now exacting my revenge by sleeping with Antonio. I should confront my unfaithful husband with this, but it is too late at this point.

I make sure to lock my bedroom door and even wedge a chair against it. Same for the terrace door. No unexpected nocturnal visitors.

29

In the late summer of 1944, among the ruins of a monastery—of which there were apparently plenty in Italy, but none at the time inhabitable or inhabited—I met a woman who had been blinded by fire from an artillery shell. It hadn't happened during this war, but during the previous one, and much further north, close to the Austrian border. In the meantime, over the past quarter of a century, she had managed to bear her lack of sight and had developed other abilities that were helping her to survive.

When I met her, she was not alone, while the dirty and exhausted Polish and British soldiers with whom I marched towards the front sought shelter for the night. She had with her a young man, sixteen or seventeen, who was not her son and not even related to her. As happens during wars and disasters, the most unlikely companions find each other. He cared for her, and he spoke English quite well, although he wouldn't say where he learned it. But he translated what she said for me.

The old woman tried to compensate her loss of sight with stories she had collected over the past two decades and managed to remember. Telling stories allowed her to invest in a world of her own instead of the one she no longer could see. I have never known the extent of her repertoire, for I knew her only for a short while. The young man was as much her pupil as her physical help, as well as the repository of her stories that would live on after her.

At some point, the young man from Calabria called her his muse. I didn't understand what that meant. Why would he call her a muse? He was not an artist, not a writer, and all he did was listen to her stories and try to memorize them. I don't believe he was capable of writing anything, not even his own name. What sort of relationship did they have? They didn't even come from the same region and belonged to a very different generation.

Although illiterate, he wasn't stupid or backward. He had a lot to tell about the meaning of stories and legends, of which he seemed to know a great deal—probably thanks to her tuition. He was conversant in the origin of myths, about the ancient gods, and about the rise of Christianity that doomed these gods to hide among the common people since they no longer dared to show themselves for what they were.

He explained to me that the nature of any story is such that the imagination involved creates a new version of the common world. That way our world, the one revealed by stories, is created over and over again. The narrator of these stories, and as such the writer, molding the reality through which people travel towards the future, whether they'd be readers or not. The gods rightly frowned on this process, as they saw themselves still as the only source of stories and myths, the only ones creating the world and being allowed to. Storytellers had now taken their position, and they were powerless to halt this progression.

The old woman had given the young man all these ideas. It was her explanation for the existence of stories and storytellers. But these storytellers, she said, also created our present cruel world full of horrors, war, and death. Why did they do this?

What compelled them? This the young man wanted to know. And he asked me, of all people. Why did the world need to contain so much ugly? So much fear and pain?

Only one oil lamp illuminated the scene in those ruins, where for a few hours the war seemed distant. The woman smiled at me when the boy translated our conversation for her, along with the questions he had asked. He listened intently to her reaction but refused to translate for me. He told me she was merely talking about narrators' lies and fabrications, at my insistence. All narratives are deceptive, and those who convey them are dishonest. This was what she said, according to the young man, although he added he didn't really understand what she meant. She often contradicted herself, he said, and this confused him. He may have misunderstood her. I didn't insist. I gave them some food from my rations and water.

When the woman heard about the Goumiers, she just sat there, offering no comment at all. Not a word passed her lips. She had undoubtably heard about atrocities committed by soldiers dressed in the most diverse uniforms.

"She seldom comments on that sort of thing," the young man told me. "She patiently listens to women who have experienced abuse when they come to see her." Sometimes these women have children; sometimes they are still children themselves. These things happen all the time. Some of these women are at the end of their tether; they want to die but lack the courage to commit suicide. They tell her, We want death. Their life is worse than death. Their children's life has become worse than death. There's no future for any of them."

"What does she tell them? What can she offer them?"

The young man avoided my gaze. "She has no answers or solutions for them. She can offer them nothing."

"What happens to them?"

"Most of them are still alive the next day," he said. "And they were still alive the following week. Some don't make it. Others simply disappear. It is simple to disappear in a country at war. The children may become orphans; we don't find out."

"You are an orphan too, aren't you?"

"Yes, yes, yes, I am an orphan because my parents were killed by a bomb. A bomb. Not because they themselves chose their fate. That's quite a difference. She tells me, there's a big difference."

"Why is that?"

"My parents did not choose their death. But these women, they still have a choice: they might want to die, but they can continue to live. It is their choice. And she tells these women: If you choose not to live, then Evil wins. She doesn't want Evil to win." He looked up at me. "And I'm sure she is correct, about not letting Evil win."

I sat next to them in that dirty old monastery, where the word of God and the holy songs of the nuns once resounded. The only sound we heard was the wind. The blind woman sat in her corner, with a ragged blanket over her. She wasn't going anywhere unless the boy helped her.

I thought about the choices I had made in my life. I thought about the choices I would undoubtedly make later in life. I wanted to talk to her, but we didn't speak the same language. The young man did his best, but at no point did I get the impression he was correctly translating what she said. I had the impression that he was merely giving me an interpretation, an approximation of what she was saying. He was sharing insights from both his own and her lives with me.

Maybe she wasn't able to help other people. Maybe all he told me was a lie. It might as well all have been a fabrication. Perhaps it hadn't been a bomb that killed his parents.

The following day, the soldiers and I moved on. The woman was still sitting in the same place where she had spent the night. The boy had been standing on a pile of stones between fog banks since the first dawn, trying in vain to see something of the landscape. As we passed him, he nodded briefly, and then we were strangers again.

30

The lack of calendars and clocks in this city bothers me. It gives me the impression that I haven't heard from Morse in too long, which might be both good and bad news. Maybe he has nothing to say to me at all. If they found my husband, I would have heard about it.

I have a copy of The Times next to me at breakfast this morning, and nothing about him or my court case is mentioned, not even in the society pages. So there's nothing to worry about, I guess. There's a lot going on in Britain, but nothing of specific interest to me. Numerous conflicts exist throughout the world, yet British society remains unfazed by many of them, as they pose no threat to its economic or political interests. British society—which along with its politicians, still believes it to be the leading nation in the world, which it no longer is. The United States has taken over that role since the war, but many British are too arrogant and too proud to acknowledge this shift. The realization will come gradually, but the British still consider themselves a special case, an impregnable island, a forbidding fortress, the leader of the Commonwealth and therefore of all of human civilization. It is an illusion from which we will soon awaken. We. As if I care about this awakening of the British nation from its megalomaniac dreams.

Of course, the Italians face the same challenges. They still maintain to speak a world-class language, as direct heirs of the Roman Empire, cultural high ground, and so on. Their awakening will be brutal, too. Italy as a nation is not taken seriously any more, actually not even when Il Duce was around. The Germans needed Italy to protect their underbelly, but they had little confidence in their fascist allies.

I read The Times and am amazed at the provincialism that permeates even this pillar of English society. Newspapers no longer offer a privileged view of the world stage, but rather of what is happening under the local church tower. This worries me to no end. It is typical for a declining society, which still maintains its dreams of world dominance while at the same time retreating in its own backyard.

But now I have my own problems to solve, as a bunch of Nazi sympathizers may come knocking down my hotel door at any moment. I need to gain the upper hand in this game as soon as possible. This is what I'll do: I will return to the house on Campo S. Angelo, keep an eye on its inhabitants, and when the woman shows up again, I'll follow her. After that, I don't know. I'll improvise.

So after breakfast I'm on my way. Venice is already fully alive by that time, with the vaporettos starting their engines and the merchants on their flat boats provisioning their stores. These boats—wrecks, mostly—carry fruits and vegetables, meat and fish, clothes, olive oil, coal, and everything a city and its inhabitants need. Boats deliver everything here, with the exception of items that handcarts or bicycles can transport through the narrow alleys. Fishing is also done in the lagoon, and even the shellfish to be served with spaghetti are harvested locally.

This city probably never really sleeps, and if it does, its slumber may be superficial. It has its own public dynamic, which even tourists notice. Much of the economic activity is in the hands of just a few guilds, much like in the Middle Ages or the Renaissance. Their members practice professions protected from outsiders. Making money, at least within this context, is only allowed with their permission and with that of the other, almost invisible, rulers of Venice. These rulers are not church prelates, but organized crime. Without the Mafia's blessing, nothing happens. Its impact on the economy and finances is as obvious as the priestly class's on souls. The church and the criminal world are the two only truly functioning parts of this society.

I arrive at the Campo. Two of the three apartments in the house have curtains hanging open. There is no movement visible. No one shows up at the windows. I probably have a long and boring day ahead of me. After an hour, I start to see the pointlessness of my position. Police officers on a stakeout receive compensation for their boredom, not me. Furthermore, my presence here is very conspicuous, which is detrimental to my element of surprise. I have to find a different strategy.

I therefore follow the trail back into the other direction: the anonymous woman, Van Rijn, Antonio. If I need to start anywhere, I'd better find Antonio.

First I try the San Simeon Piccolo church, but he is nowhere in sight. A little apprehensive, I penetrate the labyrinth of alleys behind the church, realizing that last time it was dark and I didn't pay much attention to my surroundings. Nevertheless, I continue comparing small streets and squares with my failing memory of the place. I found my way back that evening, so I should be able to locate the house where we made love. I can't ask around, not only because I'm not familiar enough with the language, but mostly because I don't know what to ask for. Anyway, the few people around eye me distrustfully, and will certainly not talk to me. I manage to order an espresso and half a liter of water in a cafe, and then I'm on my way again. The darker side of Venice is swallowing me alive.

Finally, I manage to return to San Simeon Piccolo, not having found the house. It has been a senseless undertaking. But there he is: Antonio, leaning against the fence, casual but elegant at the same time, like when I first saw him. He doesn't notice me, and I quickly look for a hiding place. That is, as I mentioned before, a ridiculous undertaking, but I don't want to be seen by him.

He doesn't seem to do anything in particular. Apparently he's just hanging around—a handsome, bored young man with nothing to do, neatly dressed though not flashy, in an attitude that conveys a certain insouciance. This square is his personal property where he feels at home; that much is clear.

After a while, he seemingly at random addresses a woman. I don't know how he does it, but he finds the only passing woman who, like me, is a foreigner, probably bored, and without a companion. Although what he does isn't actually that difficult. It takes a few moments of careful observation, I suppose, to find a suitable victim. He must be skilled at that.

But he is not always successful. The woman smiles elegantly but waves him away. He doesn't insist. Fifteen minutes later, he has found another victim. Again, the same type of woman. She stops, listens, and a little later she walks away with him.

It's magic, that easily winning charm of his, and recently I found myself under his spell. But not anymore. Now I recognize his strategy for what it is: the exploitation of the weaknesses of others.

I follow them. His focus is entirely on his partner, as it should be. She is blonde, tall and slim; I estimate her to be in her mid-forties. She can get better than him, in a social sense, but here in Venice the imagination runs wild, as I can testify. A woman, alone, perceives him as the kind of lover she can't have at home, where social rules are strict and social control even more stringent.

Antonio knows perfectly how to use this illusion to his advantage. Everything about him tells women that he is simultaneously sophisticated and pleasant to be around, that he can be superficial when they need him to be, discreet of course, but also a good conversationalist. And good in bed—because in the end that's what it comes down to.

Antonio weaves the same web of illusions as I once did in London, before the war. The men I met, in the expensive hotels or clubs or all the places I could buy my way into, knew that I was selling illusions: that they were handsome and attractive to a young woman like me, that they had power (which was true, but not over me), that money allowed them everything (it did, and I hated them for it), that an evening in my company would raise their social status, and a night with me in bed would give free rein to their sexual desires (mainly why I hated them). So Antonio is cut from the same cloth as I.

In a sense that woman is still me, I am still her. I kept her hidden in a deep and dark closet and allowed her free rein again, on occasion, here in Italy, or at least during the war. Conditions were different, of course. I earned the respect of British and Canadian soldiers not by the power of my words or with my portable typewriter as a weapon, but because I learned to use a gun and a bayonet. My most beloved weapon, that bayonet. It allows you to look your enemy straight in the eyes from a close distance when you kill him.

Usually, the most primitive motifs are the easiest to understand.

I shake my head. Take it easy there, girl. The war is over. Peace has been with us for almost ten years, at least here in Europe. Or in most of Europe. No need to revisit its horrors.

I follow Antonio and the blonde woman. A labyrinth of alleys reveals itself to me, and a little later we are in the same place where I was with him the other night. The boarding house that is not a boarding house. They enter, and a moment later I follow. I don't care about her. I care about him. She is a negligible element in this story.

I remember the room. One up. I can hear him through the door, and I can hear her. She coos excitedly. There's no reason why I should hesitate any longer. He may have locked the door, but I can deal with locked doors. When I stand in the doorway, aware that I look like an avenging angel, he glances over his shoulder, furious at the unexpected interruption. He crouches over the woman's legs, her back resting on the bed. It's an unfortunate position for him, vulnerable as he is that way. Her dress is open, her breasts are small and pale.

He swears, in Italian.

"Get out!" I shout to her. I assume she speaks English.

She rises, surprised, disturbed, uncertain about the situation. He is faster, better on his toes. He rolls off her, yanks open the drawer of the bedside table, and jumps up. A slender, slightly curved knife gleams in his right hand. It looks like a fillet knife. That is his intention: he will fillet me.

The woman runs out and manages to grab her clothes and shoes along the way. I hear her descending the stairs. Antonio stands opposite me, slightly hunched over, ready to attack. He is prepared to exact revenge on me for stealing a customer. I hold my hands out in front of me, palms down, in a gesture that should seem conciliatory but is actually defensive. Does he know who I am? Does he remember who I am? He says something in Italian that I don't understand. I shake my head. I'm not going to negotiate with him.

He lashes out with the knife and betrays his inexperience because his posture is completely wrong. He is not a street fighter, at least not a trained one. He is certainly not a soldier, either, as he is careless with his weapon and clearly overestimates his position. He is a gigolo in skimpy black pants who keeps a knife in his bedside table to impress women.

I step aside, and the knife intended for my stomach misses me. With both hands, I grab his arm and turn in the direction of his stab. He loses balance, stumbles, falls, but does not release the knife. No problem: I lash out with my right leg and kick him in the face with my sturdy British shoe. It doesn't matter where you hit someone in the face, as long as you don't do it with one of your own vulnerable body parts, like your knuckles. My shoe hits him hard.

Antonio makes a strangled sound, and at once there is blood. I take a step back, then forward again, and before he can react, I kick the knife out of his hand. It clatters against the wall before landing next to me. He clearly has no idea what happened. It all happened too quickly for him to comprehend. A moment ago I was an intruder, a woman, a potential victim. Now his face is broken, he's on the floor, and I'm crouching next to him.

"L' uomo calvo," I say. "Dove vive?"

My Italian is clear and simple; my vocabulary is limited, but that's all I need at the moment. He understands exactly what I want from him. He also understands exactly his precarious position.

"Calla Lunga S. Barnaba, sedici," he says, with some difficulty. "L'appartamento superiore."

That's all I need to know. With this information, I can take the next step. Antonio has now become useless, as far as I'm concerned. I leave him there, and he licks his wounds. At best, that's all it does.

But at worst, he comes after me because his honor is blemished. My problem is one I heard about during the war: what to do with prisoners of war when you cannot immediately evacuate them behind your lines? Usually, there is some sort of solution for this.

I think you are a useless but dangerous prisoner of war, Antonio. That's all you are to me now.

But we are no longer at war. He's just a risk I'm willing to take. Hopefully he understands that I am not an easy target.

31

Underway. The next stage towards unraveling the plot. First Van Rijn, then the dark woman. I have to work quickly before the conspiracy realizes its problems and has time to react. The news that I am in the process of seizing the initiative may spread quickly. There's nothing to be done about it. Me trying to be in command of the situation might not go unnoticed by others concerned.

It is a matter of tactics: rapid deployment of troops across the terrain leaves the enemy in the dark as to your precise plans, intentions, and progress. The Germans were excellent at that. They invented mobile warfare, so to speak, and took advantage of it during the early years of the war. Conquered half of Europa, actually.

A few years ago, the Americans and their allies attempted the same tactics in Korea, but the outcome was a debacle. Korea became the disaster it should not have been. However, I'm not going to judge the Korean problem. I rely on the knowledge I acquired on the ground here in this country.

A passerby shows me the way to the Calla Lunga S. Barnaba. Number sixteen is easy enough to find. The street is lined with modern shops, interspersed with buildings that appear equally neglected. The ease with which Antonio shared this information with me suggests that Van Rijn will no longer be found here or has never lived in that premise. It's too late, I can't turn back to my source if this information turns out to be false. But Antonio did not seem a particularly brave young man, nor inclined to defend the secrets of others with his life. He was a seducer, a small cog in the whole conspiracy. Maybe he didn't even know what this was about. So I assume he was telling the truth.

I study the building. Van Rijn, if he looks outside now, sees me standing here and is at once alarmed. He flees through a back exit. I'd rather he does not, because I won't be able to find him again. A frontal attack is out of the question, where I'm concerned. I have a better idea. I enter an alley and search for the rear entrance of the building. But everything is fully built up, and the houses probably only open onto a private courtyard. This is a problem from the fire department's point of view, and it is also a problem for me because I see no way to get into the building without passing through the front door.

I anticipate another extended vigil in a street that lacks any available shelters. There are at most a few cafes serving espresso, or wine, or where you can eat a slice of pizza. A blonde tourist like me also stands out to no end. I'm a cliché in this town. However, Van Rijn is a stranger as well, an outsider, and I would be surprised if he has many contacts with local residents. No one will whisper in his ear that his house is under surveillance. They won't whisper anything in his ear.

I wait, hang out, and finally walk into a trattoria, where I sit by the window and have some pasta pomodore with a glass of red wine. The food comes from grandmother's kitchen and is therefore exquisitely tasty, just like the wine. I eat, I drink, I observe. Then I order an espresso to justify my prolonged presence.

Men come in, eat and drink, try to ignore me, whisper among themselves, laugh, and shout at each other like men do everywhere. A few newspapers are doing the rounds, usually printed on the bizarre pink paper that is so common here. Van Rijn doesn't show up.

Halfway through the afternoon, I give up and walk back north, towards my hotel. A chilly wind rises. Winter is coming.

A telegram from Morse is waiting for me at the hotel. The lawsuit has been brought before the court. There has been an uproar on the part of my former in-laws when they were officially informed of my demands. The Metropolitan Police wants to speak to me about my husband. To them, he is still my husband. They want to know where he is.

"As if I have any idea," I say to the telegram. Morse insists, in a lengthy monologue, that I should still make my appearance in London, primarily because the involvement of the police is not a positive development. They are clearly no longer satisfied with my statements to Inspector Martinengo and his silent companion. They want to hear the whole story from my mouth.

I don't know what they want to hear. I have nothing to tell them.

I'll let Morse wait for an answer. I don't plan to travel to London either, although I'm starting to think again about how this solves at least one problem. Actually, all I need is the money, and then I'm off. I estimate I can get two or three million pounds from all these settlements combined, which will be enough to start a new life elsewhere. If necessary, under a different identity.

Another identity. I'll need that.

In the restaurant's bar, I drink tea. When I look up, I recall the saying about Mohammad and the mountain. In this case, it appears that the mountain has come to Muhammad. Van Rijn, who is sitting a few tables away from me and sipping coffee, is observing me.

32

After I left the boy, did Van Rijn meet Antonio? Did Antonio tell me anything of importance about their conspiracy? That's going to be Van Rijn's concern, not mine. I for one am concerned about the turnaround in our relationship, with him sitting here and observing me. I'm on the defensive again, bereft of initiative. I must endure this uncomfortable situation. For a couple of hours I assumed I had reversed our roles, but that appears to be a temporary illusion. I will have to fall back on another strategy, which I don't have. No plan B.

He makes no move to join or speak to me. He sits at a table, enjoying a coffee and a glass of cognac, while he quietly observes. He makes no effort to hide. His presence is frightfully oppressive. Is this the man who searched my room? That seems plausible. Our previous conversation went wrong. He made a generous offer, which I refused, thereby offending him and perturbing their plans. But he also led me, indirectly, to Antonio, his co-conspirator. Did they kill Edvardo together and make his body disappear? That may seem like a reasonable assumption. I will also disappear once I have handed over the diary. Without the diary, I am at best a dangerous witness.

I can still run away from Venice and leave the problem unresolved. But I don't know how far this conspiracy extends, in a geographical sense. Can they find me in England? Am I in danger there too? Naturally, I won't have the opportunity to confront Van Rijn with this question. Neither is he the one who makes the decisions concerning my future. There's the dark-haired woman, of course, who will have her say about me.

To my surprise, Inspector Martinengo shows up. He does this by stepping decisively into the lavish baroque salon, quickly looking around, and locating me. Yes, me. He's here for me, and so Van Rijn is in trouble—because whatever his plan, it is now disrupted by the policeman's presence.

The inspector is wearing a neat, although somewhat worn, dark blue suit, with his overcoat over his arm and his hat in his hand. "Signora Barth," he says, "a moment of your time?"

"As you wish, inspector," I say, lenient as I am towards officers of the law as long as they don't ask too many difficult questions and pose no immediate threat. "Can I offer you a coffee?"

"With pleasure."

He sits across from me, looking a little nervous. I wave to a waiter and order two coffees.

"The police in London are insisting," he says, "we talk again with you. They don't seem to believe you told us all they want to know." The coffee arrives; he drinks his black. "They requested another interview."

"Another," I say. "I've had enough of these . . . interrogations."

He slowly shakes his head, sympathizing with me. "Last time was merely a question of gathering information, about what you knew concerning your husband's disappearance. What they want now must be more comprehensive. More to the point, see? Since I have no authority over you and you are not facing any criminal charges, I cannot force you to talk to us. I can't even keep you from leaving Venice."

No criminal charges. Let us keep it that way.

"But I have my orders," he continues. "My superior advises me to have another conversation with you, as we don't want to offend the British authorities." He doesn't look like he cares a great deal about the British authorities, but he is one to follow orders.

"Your superior is aware you have no leverage over me, I assume," I say.

"That is correct," Martinengo admits. "We can only give you a few words of advice. This affair pertains to nothing but the disappearance of your husband and has nothing to do with your divorce. Which is a matter between you and . . . and your lawyers, I presume. Nothing for the police to be concerned about. Divorce is something between partners, nothing more. When issues arise between them, their life together loses its appeal. These things happen, however unfortunate."

He sounds like he's speaking from personal experience, which makes him a bit more human and even sympathetic, in my opinion. We may have a few things in common. But he will not be my ally, not at any point.

Even so, I don't desire him to be my adversary either.

"We obviously have no orders to take from the British police," he says, with disarming honesty, as if this is his greatest secret, the testimony of his defiance. He offers me a way out, that's what he does. "But when I receive instructions from my hierarchy, which I cannot ignore, then, you understand . . ."

"I am in daily contact with my solicitor," I tell him. "He also appears to believe that my presence in London is necessary. Personally, I see the matter differently."

"Why?"

"Why what?"

"Why do you see it differently?"

"Because I don't want to be confronted by my husband's relatives. Our divorce has not yet been finalized. There are still ties between them and myself, but they have never been very nice people. Indeed, you can detect the irony in my tone. They are not nice people at all. The feelings are, of course, mutual. They will do anything to hurt my case and my future. Frankly, Inspector, they will lose a lot of money on me if the divorce is granted in my favor." And of course they need to cover up Michael's sordid affair as well—a detail I'm not sharing with this police officer.

"It's always a matter of money," he says. "Love is only a temporary excuse against dissatisfaction and sometimes a remedy against loneliness. When money is involved, it certainly isn't a good excuse, as we Italians are well-aware of."

"Undoubtedly. And so I don't want to return home at once. I prefer to be here rather than in London, simply because I am in love with your city."

I try to play him through his love for Venice. Does this make me a terrible person?

He sips his coffee. "I have done my duty and will now inform my superior of your wish to remain here," he says. He rises and hands me his card. "Always at your disposal, Signora. If there's anything I can do for you . . ."

Why doesn't he arrest Van Rijn now that he's at it? Would do me a great favor. But he won't; of course he won't. I remain silent and allow him to depart. I'll keep his card for later use.

Van Rijn is not at risk of being arrested because he has disappeared.

33

The inspector, who even from a distance looks like a regular police officer and makes no effort to conceal it, may have put Van Rijn off. The gray hat and the shapeless overcoat are what give it away. The head also reflects the determination and stubbornness of a civil servant. It's remarkable how clichés consistently hold true.

My own intentions regarding Van Rijn had to give way for a moment, but now I will continue my campaign—insofar as there is one worthy of the name. I have no troops, no scouts, and no information about the terrain or the enemy's nature and strength. I have nothing, except that I am aware of at least two members of the conspiracy. Three, actually. My tenacity is the other element in this game, and not an unimportant one.

However, I now realize that handing over the diary will not make me safer. On the contrary. No one needs to teach me the thorough ruthlessness of the Nazis and their followers—and these individuals are followers, if not worse. I will vanish as soon as I present myself with the diary.

Perhaps Morse will send me a telegram today, urging my immediate departure to our capital, but I will not respond. There is no accusation against me, either in London or in this case, so my court appearance is not crucial. My preference is to stay in Venice for the time being, but without the extra intrigues in which I am involved. It's a vain hope, of course. I could steer Inspector Martinengo to investigate Van Rijn's activities, potentially leading to an international conspiracy or even murder. However, the inspector will likely argue that no crime has occurred, particularly if no body is found, such as Edvardo's, and therefore he cannot take any action.

However, I have crossed a threshold myself, and my opponents will have discovered this by now because of my episode with Antonio. It depends on how they perceive me—as a conceited and vain rich woman or a hardened veteran of several battles. Or something in between. Their further actions will depend on this vision. How well do they know me? What do they know about me? Do they really believe Antonio when he tells them that I was able to overwhelm him almost effortlessly? If the answer to that question is positive, then they will be inclined to approach me with caution. And I hope, with respect.

Is that why Van Rijn waited for me at the hotel?

To approach me with caution and respect?

Let him come. I'll have to keep those opponents on the line for a while longer—mainly because I want to know how strong they are. I want to discover the number of their allies and the extent to which they have infiltrated official circles, such as the police. If all this concerns a powerful fascist network at the heart of the Italian government and law enforcement agencies, I'm in deep trouble. They will have people who can make me talk—wasn't that what Van Rijn said? Given their history and backgrounds, I have no doubts about his intentions.

I do what is expected of me: I spend my time doing more sightseeing. There are a few bookstores I pop into, just to run my fingers along all those almost illegible spines. I would like to buy a book by D'Annunzio but cannot find an English edition. Obviously, no Italian bookseller would betray the memory of one of their most beloved writers by providing translations. This would be unheard of.

I even avoid checking if I'm being followed. I am meant to be followed. And so I turn my attention to Venice. As far as I am concerned, it is a cryptic city because I am unable to decipher the language of its alleys and streets, as I can in London and Paris, two cities for which I do not need a Baedeker or a city map.

34

Van Rijn is standing in front of me while two other men are hanging around nearby, watching me. All three wear appropriate city clothes with a dark overcoat and hat. They belong together, and they will get physical if needed, that much is clear. Van Rijn says, "Get in, Mrs. Barth." He gestures toward the dock, where a motorboat waits, with a fourth man behind the wheel. Another sullen-looking man. The conspiracy clearly has some resources at its disposal. They are not amateurs.

I don't even consider escaping. I have taken care of Antonio, but these three men are on a different level entirely. They look professional, probably ex-military. They will use force if necessary. Do I shout for help? Seems hopeless. There are hardly any people around. No one will come to my aid or call the police.

The men are polite and forthcoming. They assist me in boarding the motorboat and entering the cabin, where they have drawn the curtains in front of the windows while only a few wall fixtures are lit. They don't want anyone to see me, and they don't want me to see where they're taking me. Mind you, this is not a kidnapping: Van Rijn invited me in an almost friendly fashion. Old friends and all that. No coercion or threat.

Technically, they are not committing a crime. But I have no illusions: if I don't come along, they will use violence.

"Can I inquire about our destination? And what is the purpose of this, er, trip?"

Van Rijn sits opposite me on a bench running along the boat's length. The boat is luxurious, with expensive attributes like shiny wood, brass, leather, and copper. What does that tell me about the people who use it? It may be rented, I assume. Expensive, but still rented.

"There is someone who wants to speak with you, Mrs. Barth," says Van Rijn, not above avoiding the cliché. The other two men don't appear to be interested in our conversation. However, they are closely monitoring me. I won't be able to unexpectedly surprise them, even if I plan to do so. They are my age, maybe a little older, German rather than Italian, and probably served during the war. If they are in the company of a man like Van Rijn, it is not difficult to guess what kind of uniform they wore. And they're not going to make the mistake of underestimating me. Not like Antonio did.

Poor, wretched Antonio, who fancied himself a hero but couldn't even subdue me. Did he see himself as the reincarnation of the young heroes from this city's history? Plenty of historical examples. Too many illusions for such a young boy.

I'm not going to try anything. Not right here on this motorboat, at least. I want to find out who wants to meet me so urgently. I am eager to see the faces of those involved in this plot. For instance, I would like to reveal the identity of the primary organizer of this conspiracy. Seems like a good idea to keep my mouth shut and see how things develop.

The motorboat makes a slow turn to the right. I can hear the engine's steady hum and the splash of water against the hull. I hear a passing seagull calling out plaintively. Occasionally the curtains move slightly, but not enough to give me a view of the surroundings. Our destination remains a mystery to me. That means—maybe—they want to bring me back alive.

Or at least somewhat alive. Perhaps excluding a few parts, not of an essential nature or necessary for my further survival, and only detrimental to my aesthetic appearance. It is said—something I heard in North Africa—that the sight of your own finger being amputated (not to mention the pain) changes many people's minds. An amputated toe evokes the same reaction. Or nose.

We haven't been out on the water for very long when the sound of the engine changes pitch. The vessel slows down and begins to move to the right. The engine is switched off. I can hear voices outside. The sound of the hull briefly hitting a wooden quay. The splashing of water. After that, there is only the silence of the lagoon.

"We have arrived," Van Rijn announces. "Let's get off board, Mrs. Barth."

We are still in Venice, presumably on one of the isolated islands.

35

We walk along a stone quay. Its construction dates back to historical times, ancient Roman even, perhaps, and it has undergone frequent restorations. This was not always done judiciously, sometimes with brick, sometimes with concrete of a rather poor quality. Often it looks like shoddy work, unworthy of this city and its historical legacy. This is clearly not a popular mooring spot, not intended for tourists, with only two motorboats of the same type as the one we arrived with and some flat freight barges like those that use the Canale Grande to supply the city center. On the quay two former German trucks, still in their now faded feldgrau color, are parked, both with a crane to hoist goods from quay to boat and vice versa. There's no one around. Further on, I see houses and trees, part of a wooded area. I look behind me and see the somewhat foggy, dreamy lagoon and, in the distance, the vaguely outlined silhouette of Venice. From this viewpoint, the city seems to want to disappear into the water, never to emerge again.

"Mrs. Barth," says Van Rijn, preceding me. Only the pilot remains in the boat; the two other men follow us. They are still observant, even though I can't go anywhere. Escape is out of the question, unless I want to swim.

Van Rijn behaves oddly, as if he is not fully comfortable with this situation and his role in this affair. As if he would rather not be here and has been developing second thoughts recently. Today, he wears a hat to protect himself from the chill, but it doesn't suit him well.

We walk down the quay. At the end is a street lined with wide, gray flagstones that runs up a hill, passing by several houses surrounded by cypresses and plane trees. The houses are large and appear to be well maintained, each on its own extensive plot of land. They will undoubtedly be owned by members of the upper class. No densely populated neighborhood here. No peeling facades and rotting window frames. No clothes hanging to dry or chatting grandmothers in flowered aprons. No eateries with pizza and red wine in two-liter bottles. No fried sardines or boiled vegetables. The neighborhood can only be defined by its absences.

Van Rijn precedes me up the hill. The street is narrow, but just wide enough for a car. In front of one of the houses, a new-looking black sedan from a well-known Italian brand has been carelessly parked. The island is probably not an island but is connected to the mainland. Unless the car got here on a ferry.

Van Rijn walks along a tiled driveway to a wide door on the side of the house. A middle-aged woman of medium stature, wearing a neat gray apron, opens the door. She casually nods at Van Rijn and steps back. She doesn't say a word. We all walk inside.

The house is lavishly furnished and decorated with great taste. Most of the furniture is modern, Bauhaus or Art Deco or whatever, and kept in excellent condition. Not exactly my style. Colorful, abstract paintings hang on the walls in the spacious hall and in the adjoining salon, which I can partly see through an open double door. There are no Canalettos or other classical masters on exhibit here.

In an armchair by the wide window of a veranda overlooking a deep, green garden, sits a man in white trousers, a powder-blue shirt, and a white jacket. Very elegant; that much is at once clear. He is a man with impeccable fashion sense. I assume he is the master of the house. And I'm here for this man.

He rises to his feet and beams at him.

It's my husband.

36

My husband. My faithless, pedantic, and meddlesome husband. Soon to be my ex-husband. Whom I have never seen in this kind of clothing, except very exceptionally during a rare summer garden party. A real British party, with the obligatory game of cricket, Pimm's and Champagne, cakes, and strawberries with whipped cream. On such few occasions he would get dressed up like this.

Allow me to introduce him, if I haven't already: Michael Holzman-Smith, with that famous double surname. Here he is, making an unexpected yet grand appearance. Especially unexpected. And equally extremely unwelcome, as far as I'm concerned.

Because the problem is this: I killed him in London.

Let me explain. Let me share here, at this moment, a few details and a story about my wonderful plan, as it should have developed over there in the British capital. And I promise, this time, to tell as much of the truth as possible.

Let's move back to London, two weeks ago. Or a little less than two weeks—I've lost sense of time and the passage of time, which is what Venice does to you. Venice manipulates and compresses time, transforming it into peculiar forms. Past and present and so on, not always easy to distinguish. Just as it is difficult to tell the different days and nights apart.

It's been approximately two weeks. The case against my husband for infidelity and sodomy is being prepared by the court, which may want to convene behind closed doors out of respect for his family. But mainly because the common people do not need to know what the elite is up to in those castles and mansions. The elite would rather not see all those juicy stories discussed extensively in newspapers and pubs.

Master Morse has completed his dossier and written the necessary letters to my husband on the one hand and his family on the other. These letters clearly explain my position (the deceived and humiliated wife) and the details of what I expect in compensation (half of his assets and a large chunk of the wealth of his family, which I accuse of having hidden his true nature from me and thus to have allowed me to marry him with fraudulent motives. Let them try to debunk that argument, *dixit* Master Morse).

So far, all seemed to go well for me. The young man with whom I caught my spouse in bed was willing to put his confession on paper and to provide me with the letters my husband wrote to him. Yes, those horny letters. He wanted to escape his punishment, or at least hoped for a lenient judge in his own case. Master Morse would—in a separate trial—take up his defense and deflect all blame onto my husband. The young man would—as I explained earlier—not completely escape justice, but he would certainly not be subjected to the maximum punishment and maybe not even see the inside of His Majesty's prisons. I would generously compensate him afterwards.

Such was the deal. Everything seemed neatly arranged. Master Morse was convinced that I need not worry about the outcome of the case. *Really nothing to worry about, Mrs. Barth.*

Of course he was good at talking, that being his job. He guided me to the entrance of his office, navigating past the youthful-appearing solicitors which he usually kept on a short leach. They might eventually find their own place in the legal system, or they might not, depending on their talents. I recognized their hungry look, which I had experienced with much older men while I undressed in front of them. It's as if men can only display that hungry look on the way to their doom, because women as well as material aspirations often lead to their downfall. They rarely realize this until it's too late, if at all. Men are pathetic.

But let us return to the story.

Naturally, my husband and his solicitors confronted me about my claims. I took great care to distance myself from him and relocated my belongings to an apartment I rented under my own name, but with his money. However, I couldn't avoid him all the time. We had a few, not always private, run-ins. On such occasions, harsh words and even threats were uttered, but I knew he and his family wanted to keep everything out of the newspapers. With a court case, this would be a major problem for them. At least he made an effort to avoid publicizing our arguments too frequently.

But one day Michael confronted me about my claims to a share of his fortune. He literally said he wouldn't share a penny with a whore like me. He told me to forget about the whole arrangement, and his family would not pay me anything once they discovered the truth about who I really was.

Who I was.

Who I had been.

When I had been someone other than his wife.

And I realized he *knew*.

Somehow he knew (and had recently acquired this knowledge,

I assumed). Somebody had informed him about my pre-war activities and about my shameful life as an escort. I had drastically changed my appearance, making it seem unlikely that anyone from those days would have recognized me. But there were still too many similarities between myself and that smart, enterprising woman from back then, who scoured the city's best hotels in borrowed ball gowns. For one thing, it's impossible to alter your voice.

How Michael came to know about my past doesn't really matter. He had the means, he said, to prove in court what a dishonorable profession I had been pursuing. He would state that he was unaware of my past and therefore would argue that I had deceived him, rather than the other way around. There would have been no marriage if he had known who I really was. Consequently, my arguments would no longer be valid. He would instead, he said, burn me to the ground. He would have witnesses called to testify against me, and so on.

The question can easily be asked why he had not checked my antecedents earlier, by a specialized private detective, before our marriage. Wasn't that a common practice in his midst? Or had he been blinded by my reputation as a brave and notorious journalist who had written excellent in-depth war stories, sometimes even compared with Ernest Hemingway and Martha Gellhorn? Did the young woman fearlessly venture into the core of the conflict?

Wasn't he surprised or disturbed by the great black hole that made up the rest of my past, as well as the fact that he never met any of my family? Did he simply accept the story that I had shared with them about how insignificant my pre-war years had been?

I could at that point live with the situation: I was not going to reveal the part of my past that I wanted to cover up at all costs, nor was I critical of his past itself. I assumed he wanted me out of some kind of blind love—although that thought proved a bit naive. As far as he was concerned, I was exactly the kind of woman he needed: famous and yet an enigma, someone with whom he could shock his own family and friends because I was not of the same class, and I often moved in the wrong circles.

Now, however, I was confronted with this new development. The concealing veil had been torn away from my past. The slut, who had once been sold for a few pieces of silver, now stood naked before him and the public. Was his haughty family aware of this grotesque development? Had he told them what he had found out about me?

No, he told me, he hadn't done that. Yet. But he would not hesitate to expose me if I continued the current state of affairs concerning the lawsuit.

Which was, in itself, an interesting development and, of course, a mistake on his behalf. The secret was still safe, for the time being, as far as his family and the rest of society were concerned. And the witnesses he would call up would only appear when Michael guaranteed them protection. Otherwise, I assumed, they would not want to go public on the unsavory things they themselves did before the war.

This gave me the opportunity to change the situation to my advantage. Michael was the only person standing in my way. In my experience during wartime, I had learned that almost any object, even the more common ones, can be turned into a deadly weapon. In addition, I had acquired several techniques for making a body vanish. All of that might yet proves to be useful.

The matter, however, was one of opportunity. If I wanted to make Michael disappear, would I have to do that myself? The logistics of such a process were not very obvious. I needed a specialist for such matters. But first of all, I needed time.

He agreed to a reprieve. He would wait with his revelations, giving me time to consider my position. This suited me fine, and it sealed his fate.

<h1 style="text-align:center">37</h1>

I had (and still have) quite a few connections from my time in Italy during the war. The special thing about military conflicts is the bond with your companions, those who stand next to you while an enemy tries hard to kill you. It is this bond that helps make the cruelty, the slaughter, death, and mutilation bearable. It's a bond for life.

But it is an exclusive bond. Old fighters find only misunderstandings in the society to which they return. Anyone who has known the stench of death has lived a different life and spent that life (or the most intense part of it) in a different place. Those who remain at home cannot comprehend this.

No one really comes back from war intact. Often, the mind suffers more than the body. Those who returned after the war and sought a place in society would sooner or later rely on that bond with former soldiers to find support and understanding. Strangers have become brothers. They substitute for family members. The dead, those who didn't make it, are rarely talked about. The dead are not held accountable. However, the living developed a sense of obligation towards one another.

I knew, and still know, many former soldiers. I contacted one of them in a not very reputable London pub. He was a man I could rely on, or so I assumed. We had a pint, or something else; I don't remember exactly. We conversed about nothing in particular, or perhaps we remained silent and simply enjoyed the quiet. After a while, I explained to him what I needed to be done. What he could do for me. And what I was willing to pay for. I didn't tell him everything, just what he needed to know.

They all need money, those former soldiers, even ten years after the war. There is persistent poverty in England. There is a lot of hidden poverty. There is unemployment, especially among veterans. This man possessed qualities that I wanted to put to use. I had enough money, so I was willing to reimburse him for his special effort.

For his part, he was willing to engage in activities that others tend to avoid. He already had done that in Italy. And even before the war, in England, he hadn't always been a nice person. He didn't say much about those days while we were in Italy, but he hinted plenty. He was a man I wouldn't have met under other circumstances. We would have inhabited different worlds.

And now we were sitting at a table in a pub somewhere in the not-so-reputable Soho. And we hatched a plot.

I don't want to detail my story. In any case, I am not going to name names or quote details, for reasons that will become evident later. I approached him with a financial proposal, aware of his precarious situation and that of his family. The proposal was about money. Upon his death, my lawyer would provide a lifetime annuity to him and his family. In return, I asked him not to do more than what he had done often enough in Italy.

He had to take a life.

38

"Oh," Michael says in that teasing tone of his, "I understand perfectly; I always did. I understand your confusion. You wonder what happened to me and to that friend of yours, that shady and—let's be honest—not very trustworthy friend from your infamous military days. You're taken aback to find me here, as you had anticipated that my remains would be buried beneath a thick layer of concrete. Or whatever. That clearly didn't happen. I am still alive and in excellent health, thank you. Well, that's what happens when you let others do your dirty work, Ellen. My treacherous and lying Ellen. You were in the army—or nearly so, because you've never really been a soldier, right? You *played* soldier in the Sahara and in Italy. Didn't they teach you to do your own dirty work? If you want to execute a deserter, you do it yourself, especially if you are an officer. You've heard of those kinds of rules about honor and masculinity that everyone keeps talking about, right? No one is served by someone else's shoddy work. But you do, apparently. To make a long story short, my dear Ellen: I offered more money. It's that simple."

"That seems too easy," I say. But yes, here he is. He's not dead.

"Indeed, it wasn't as simple as it seemed, to tell the truth. There was more to it than just money. He and I engaged in a robust discussion about the ramifications of a homicide on a member of my social group. If they found out about him, he would be hanged. Also, all this is your fault, by the way, because you expected that the man you sent after me, with whom you shared I don't know what in Italy—that very same man would just kill me because you asked him and offered money for it. So we had that conversation, and he understood where his interests lay, especially since he would get paid twice for the same non-effort. By me.

"He informed you afterwards that I was dead, my body had disappeared forever, and you could pretend that you knew nothing because you were already on your way to Venice. You had a solid alibi. After that, you could persuade people I would have—I don't know, maybe gone into hiding? Wasn't that the scenario you had in mind? Something that would discredit me in the eyes of the judge and jury while actually being dead? Decent plan, but not very nice on your part. Things turned out differently, woman. Did you really think you could outsmart me?"

I remain silent. What can I say? I have nothing more to say. I hate him. I hate him now more than ever. Because he messed up my careful plan. Because I did not manage to outsmart him.

"And what happens now? That's what you're wondering. Because now I am here, in Venice, and you are here as well. The two of us. Well, we're just going to have to turn the tables, won't we? You disappear, and I pop back up in London. What do you think—isn't that a wonderful idea? And a credible story, too. I really needed to go somewhere to recharge my batteries, or whatever they call it, but now I'm back. And I'll sound credible with that explanation for my absence. I can sound very credible if I want to.

"And that witness of yours? That boy you caught in my bed? Do you really think he's going to testify in court if you don't show up? Because you won't show up, Ellen. Be sure of that. You don't show up anywhere. We can make it happen by accident. Nothing is easier to arrange than an accident. Accidents just happen here in Venice. Often enough, and to careless tourists. They drink too much, tumble into the canal, and drown. While it's unfortunate, very few people will regret whatever happens, in your case."

I take a look at Van Rijn. He doesn't look at me. He is not interested in this matter, or he wants to remain neutral. He tries very hard to remain neutral, even if it's clear what my husband is talking about.

"Don't expect any help from him, Ellen," says Michael, who has followed my gaze. "Do you know why he's here? He's here because he's upset at you. He's here because you still have something he wants from you. You were so stubborn not to accept his earlier proposal. Stupid of you. Really stupid of you. Why didn't you just do as he asked? Why didn't you just give him the diary? It would have made some things way easier. That diary isn't your problem, is it, Ellen? Now you're making enemies you can't afford."

"You can't understand about the diary, Michael."

"Really not? I too fought the Nazis."

"Yes. Because you were a professional soldier. I wasn't. I didn't even *have* to fight."

He huffs indignantly. He's pretty fucked up, that husband of mine, he who has no soul and even less of a heart. "And that suddenly gives you more rights, or what?" he ripostes. "Moral rights or whatever they are?"

I can tell him that the war required a commitment from me that *he* was not prepared to give. He was there to honor his homeland and represent his family. He's that crazy. I was there to report, to show the world the madness of human civilization and the cruelty of political discourse. I wonder which of us succeeded best.

But does it mean I'm morally superior to him?

"What is your business with him?" I ask, nodding at Van Rijn. "What do you have to do with those fascists? And with that diary?"

He glances at Van Rijn. "Maybe that's too complicated for you to understand, Ellen," he says.

That's what he always does. Downplaying everything I do. I'm a woman, so the things men do are too complex for me. I am a woman and therefore intellectually inferior.

"Just try it," I suggest.

"The ideas associated with fascism are not entirely objectionable. There are certain concepts . . . What I mean is this: Nazism and fascism as they developed in Germany and Italy from the 1920s onwards must be seen within the context of that time. They were attractive to people who felt betrayed by foreign powers after the end of the first war, who had their fill of the established political order, and who lived in extreme poverty. Fascism was a natural way forward for them. The Nazis in Germany promised safety, food on the table, and jobs. They delivered. The way things eventually turned out, with the war and the persecution of Jews and all, was completely wrong, I admit. I'm not going to whine about that. All those excesses . . . Nationalism must not result in the destruction of other cultures and mass deaths."

"No, that would be detrimental to the global economy."

He ignores my sarcasm. "It was destined to lead towards capitalism, which it ultimately did. Other cultures must recognize the bright and alluring light of right-wing capitalism for what it is: their only viable future. Our true enemy, both that of fascism and of liberal democracy, is communism. That much we knew before the war broke out. However, it seems today communism is gaining ground on the values of Western civilization, on the values of Europe. The more enlightened minds of the fascist movements predicted this evolution thirty years ago. They knew that Stalin and his ilk had to be stopped because they would only settle for total world dominance. These enlightened minds included figures like Hitler and Göring, but not Himmler and Goebbels. These were hardly intellectuals. They did not understand how to defend Europe's ideas against the barbarians from the East. They were misled by their irrational hatred of the wrong groups in society. But Hitler understood, as did many others. And today the same thing is happening again . . ."

"Is that why you want to get your hands on that diary?"

"Don't underestimate the power of such symbols, Ellen. The masses need a symbol. They believe in symbols rather than in complex ideas."

"Oh, and you are now friends with these Nazis?"

"What do you want, Ellen? What do you all want, you bleeding liberal souls? The end of civilization, with everyone under the thumb of communism? Sovjets in Paris and London? Is that it? And by the way, I'm not concerned about this diary. At most, I just want to do my friends here a favor."

He gets excited, just a little too much, that husband of mine. This conversation does not promise to evolve in the right direction, especially because it is bogged down in regrettable clichés. I glance at the other men, who stand by indifferently but attentively. Like a guard of honor. Give them each an armband with that terrible symbol, white, black, and red, and there we are again, like twenty years ago. This villa indicates the involvement of a higher class in this plot. Is this their temporary headquarters? Or did they just rent this place? Just for this meeting?

"So you're associating with this new version of fascism," I

say. "Glad to hear that. However, I am still unable to discern any connection between them and you. Except for the shared sympathies."

His expression does not bode well. "Ellen, Ellen, I already told you that this is too complex for your limited intellectual capabilities. I have been actively involved in these areas for some time now. Not Nazism, mind you, but the ranks of those who are disinclined to the excesses of Marx's teachings. Who does not believe in the kind of communal spirit advocated by our former allies in the Soviet Union? The rest is coincidence. You're starting this absurd lawsuit against me because you're dissatisfied with some of the liberties I took."

"You fucked . . ."

". . . and while that case was taking its course, I was notified by friends that you had received a letter from someone they were interested in. The man you know as Edvardo, who wanted to offer you Alfred Rosenberg's diary. No doubt he trusted your reputation as a journalist. A very dubious affair, actually, but I knew at once your journalistic intuition would have been awakened. I knew you would respond because I am aware of your stubbornness. So you left for Venice. A good idea, it seemed to me. And then, in London, this old friend of yours shows up—this soldier. With a plan to expedite me to Valhalla.

"I at once knew what I was going to do. I understood how to turn your weapons against yourself. I knew exactly which fate I would reserve for you. You went to Venice because you couldn't resist the allure of a mystery. You left the trial in the hands of Master Morse, who had told you that a short vacation would do you good. Meanwhile, I wanted to discredit you because it was the only way I would win the lawsuit. Destroying your reputation in court was what I had in mind. But my new friends also really wanted to get their hands on the diary. Maybe we could combine both plans . . . And so, here we are."

"Meanwhile," I say, "you still don't have the diary, and you would go to court with a story about your sudden disappearance, which no one would be inclined to believe."

Michael shakes his head. Suddenly his eyes look sad, but I am convinced he does not regret my fate. "Initially, my intention was to turn your plan completely against yourself, Ellen. You would disappear here in Venice. A sad but shady affair, actually. Something rather suspicious. Your body would never be found. And no link to me. It seemed like such an intriguing idea: that you would literally cease to exist. But in the meantime, I have a much better idea. You don't actually have to disappear. You don't have to have an accident here. Because I have a much worse fate in mind for you, Ellen. The kind of fate that better suits your evil intentions for me."

"What might that be?"

"Murder, Ellen. You have murder on your conscience. Here in Venice. And for that you will hang, maybe even literally, but not after going through the shame of a lawsuit."

39

A murder. Antonio. They killed him because he knew too much, and now they're making me pay for it. They will pin this on me, and then I will indeed hang. Literally, because just like in the United Kingdom, the death penalty still exists in Italy, so the noose awaits here too. At the same time, this significantly reduces my chances of receiving financial compensation from Michael and his family. This severely limits my future. Even Master Morse can't help me because he probably can't intervene in an Italian court. At best, he can find me a decent Italian lawyer.

And such a court will not spare me, despite the fact that I am a woman. I killed a young Italian. I smothered a young life—that will be the conclusion of the investigating detectives. Indeed, I have visited Antonio's room, leaving traces of my presence there. I left prints all over the place.

I will try to maintain my innocence, but perhaps I would be better off pleading self-defense. However, I should not have left the scene of the crime but have called the police immediately. Although, when I left, Antonio was still alive. I didn't hang around, so I'm suspect. And don't tell us, Signora Barth, that this was a crime of passion, because the boy was known as a gigolo who seduced rich older ladies for money. At most, I can argue that I killed him out of shame. But will that help?

Michael has the matter under control; that much is clear. I played to his advantage. I blindly played the cards he wanted to see played, and I lost. Without Antonio, he would have had a much more difficult time getting out of the trial in London. Now, I offered him the solution on a silver platter. My severed head on a silver platter, actually.

The Italian police will arrest me shortly, and I will go to jail awaiting trial here in Venice. Meanwhile, a pompous British judge grants my divorce, ensuring I never see a penny from Michael or his family. That, I assume, is the plan.

It's even worse: Michael is counting on the Italian judge to hand down the death penalty. Then, I will be permanently removed from his life. There will be no case against him. And my blood isn't even on his hands.

Meanwhile, we're all here together, in the salon of a lavish villa somewhere on the Venetian archipelago. The game isn't played out yet. I hope I can find a few things up my sleeve.

"And what happens now?" I inquire.

"It all depends on that somewhat slow inspector Martinengo," says Michael. I'm not surprised he knows the police officer's name. He is apparently familiar with many pieces of the puzzle. He has his sources here. "As an Italian police officer, one can assume he will do the right thing when an easily solved murder falls into his lap. With a witness who has seen the potential murderer of the poor young fellow. But he will have to do everything by the book, so I guess you still have another day or so of freedom. Not much more than that. Maybe some investigating judge will act a little faster, and Martinengo will be ordered to arrest you today. Then, you will spend the next few nights in a cell."

"And I will stay here until . . ."

He smiles calmly and engagingly. That's how I know him: disarmingly charming, when he knows he has things under control. When everything goes his way. "No, we'll return you to your hotel. We grant you a few more hours of apparent freedom. My friends will make sure you don't run away."

I don't understand why we came all this way here. Perhaps Michael aimed to impress me by demonstrating the complete control that certain powerful forces have over this game. I am, however, not completely convinced of that game. This villa is a piece of decor, and that's all it is. It is proof of his vanity, of his ostentation. This vanity is one of his more distinguishable qualities, all of which suit Venice so well. He wants to prove something—maybe his influence and how far it reaches—but I don't care.

Van Rijn steps closer. He looks at me impassively. I turn around without giving Michael another glance. Certainly not the look of fear he expects. I don't grant him that. I'm following Van Rijn. We leave the villa and advance over the quay. A weak sun makes its appearance in between dark clouds and covers the surroundings in an almost surreal light, which suits my mood. Or not. It feels like I'm already walking towards the scaffold.

But we're not there yet. Far from.

The curtains of the boat are now open. It doesn't matter anymore. I can tell Martinengo the whole story, but he didn't seem like a man with much imagination or empathy. The story isn't exactly believable either. Kidnapped by men in black, victimized by my cheating husband, framed for a murder I didn't commit? No, no one is going to believe me.

The return journey to Venice takes place in silence. It is quickly getting dark. I have nothing more to ask Van Rijn, and he keeps his mouth shut, perhaps out of respect for my problems. But the men in the cabin don't lose sight of me. They seem to consider me dangerous, with so little left to lose. But there are four of them, so I keep a low profile.

Once on land, I can go. They don't take me back to the hotel; they don't follow me; apparently I can go wherever I want. I can take the train straight to Austria or Switzerland, but I probably won't pass border control. Martinengo will be aware of my case and will make sure I don't get far.

Time for me to come up with another plan.

40

I pass the hotel's reception. A young man and two young women are present, but they ignore me. My quasi-anonymity endures. I still have the key to my room in my pocket, and my stuff seems untouched. Everything is neatly in its place, as it was before. Nobody waits for me, handcuffs ready. No Carabinieri appear in the hallway and deny me access to the room. No inspector Martinengo to arrest me. For now, it looks like everything is going on as usual. However, what does "usual" mean to me?

For a moment, I toy with the thought that Michael might just want to scare me. His story is nothing more than a way to put pressure on me. He and his companions refrained from approaching the police, fearing that they could be implicated in the death of a certain young Venetian. Their presence in the city might raise a number of awkward questions.

So maybe there's nothing going on at all. Michael is using a devious ploy to keep me here, ensuring my appearance in a London court is avoided. Does this make sense? Such a plan probably has a high rate of success. Without my presence in the British capital, my case would collapse due to the absence of a crucial witness. Isn't that precisely what Morse cautioned me against?

On the other hand, Michael's absence is a matter of concern. However, his lawyers will present the court with a credible explanation, portraying him as a victim rather than a perpetrator. The judge will be inclined to accept that statement as true, given Michael's social standing. Contrasted with my social standing—not to mention my past—he's a saint. I am the fallen woman, the golddigger, the witch who's after the money of a naïve man foolish enough to marry her and accept her in his family. All naïve and innocent people, and certainly more believable than I.

That's how British justice works for the likes of me.

But right now, standing in my expensive hotel room, I'm in a vacuum. I don't know what my next step is going to be. I could try to call Morse, but maybe he's not in his office right now. I question his ability to manage the situation, which has spiraled out of control. I doubt whether I still have his sympathy, and I probably don't deserve it. And without him, I'm completely in the dark.

However, why should I consider Michael's story credible? He clearly managed to come to some arrangement with the man whom I sent to kill him; that much is certain. Perhaps that same man could also testify against me, though I doubt it. But he may show up, play the remorseful criminal and potential murderer who has actually not committed a crime, and the court would allow his testimony against me. If I'm not going to be convicted in Venice for murder, then I'm bound to face a charge in Londen for attempted and for conspiracy to. I'll probably hang.

I have to face it: the whole situation does not look favorable for me.

I lie down on my bed fully clothed. After a few minutes, I discover I am hungry. Despite my problems, my body continues to function normally. It needs food, and anything somewhat decent will do. Outside, night has fallen, silent but inevitable. I don't remember when I last ate today. Breakfast, I assume.

I quickly take a shower and put on different clothes: tight black trousers, sturdy boots, a black blouse, a sweater, and my leather jacket. I look in the mirror. Venice won't be safe tonight, but this may be my last free night for a very long time.

I am not the only one strolling around the streets. It isn't really cold yet, and tourists enjoy their carefree walks along the Grand Canal, have a warm drink on a heated terrace, and visit shops. Yet everyone is dressed warmly, with woolen overcoats, hats, scarves, and gloves. It's all rich people, of course, as the poor and the needy stay hidden from these parts of Venice.

The tourists are proof of the attraction of Venice as a destination for the well-to-do. Nevertheless, the former maritime republic has always kept a certain distance from whatever happened on the mainland, and this attitude is still noticeable today. Venice has always been suspicious of anyone who did not have a strong bond with the sea. When the Venetians felt obliged to fight on land, they mainly did so with the aid of foreign mercenaries. Their own soldiers and officers mainly served in their impressive navy.

I am, however, no longer a tourist. Not in this former maritime republic, where even time and the passage of time are relative, depending on the season. I wasn't a tourist before, but then I could afford to look at the city unhindered and enjoy its beauty. I've come to the realization that future walks of this nature will be beyond my reach. At least when Michael gets his way. Perhaps I should ask Saint Mark in the basilica for his intervention. The saint seems to have rarely abandoned the Venetians. Too bad I'm not a believer. Marcus is not going to step down from the heavens to offer me a solution to my problems.

41

But Edvardo does. He does pop up at the most unexpected and unguarded moment. Not from heavens, but he's here, nonetheless.

Although not in the literal sense. The following morning, I stand in front of a store, admiring the display of leather gloves for both sexes, wallets, belts, and other expensive items, more out of boredom than curiosity, as I have no intention of making any purchases at this time. As if Saint Mark, from whom I expect no help, intervenes, a girl appears next to me. I estimate her age to be no more than ten. She is dressed neatly but simply, and it doesn't look like she's begging. "*Signora,*" she says, kindly, decisively. "*Mi viene inviato da un amico.*"

A friend. She is sent by a friend? A friend of mine?

"*Chi è quell' amico?*" I say, in my best Italian.

"*Signore Edvardo. Ha detto che avresti pagato.*"

I know that last word. I assume she desires payment from me. To take me to Edvardo.

I put my hand in my jacket's pocket in search of money, which I always carry with me.

"*No, non qui!*" she says quickly. "*Andiamo!*"

And away she strides, convinced that I will follow her. That the bait is sufficiently appetizing to get me moving.

Edvardo?

Who, when I last saw him, didn't look particularly well. Whom I now imagine to be dead, which is unfortunate, but then again he chose the wrong side of history, and he is partly responsible for some of my current problems. On the other hand, he is not among those who wished me harm, and so he was a potential ally.

I follow the small figure. Alleys, alleys, more alleys. Dusk regains the upper hand over light, even during the day. The pleasant part of the city is soon behind us. She halts at a porch with a partially open door. She nods towards the door and, at the same time, holds up her right hand to me. I peel three bills from a stack and hand them over. All things considered, it is a significant amount of money. She looks delighted and immediately flees the scene. Afraid that I will change my mind and demand some of the money back?

Inside, some weak, dusty electric bulbs burn in a hollow, chilly hallway. I find an open door, painted injudiciously purple. The room behind it is equally dimly lit, with hardly any furniture except for three stern chairs and a table. Against the wall is a sink with a tap and a gas fire. The kettle is on. A large window, not particularly clean, with a view of rooftops.

Edvardo is standing at the sink. He looks better than last time. He is still alive, for one thing. He turns the knob on the stove, and the flame extinguishes. Then he pours hot water into a teapot, waits a moment, slowly moves the teapot back and forth, and fills two mugs from it. Finally, he brings the mugs to the table. With a barely perceptible movement of his head, he invites me to sit down. There's no milk or sugar.

"Where is the diary?" he asks, without further ado.

Straight to the heart of the matter, doesn't he? As far as he is concerned, this is the most pressing and the most logical question. He risked his life for the diary, and it would still be valuable to him, and as such, I understand his interest. He doesn't care much for me, on the other hand. I might be disposable.

"Safely put away," I tell him. I'm not going to ask what happened to him after he brought me the diary at the hotel, and about who was responsible for his situation at that time.

"Safe?" he echoes. He pushes one steaming mug towards me.

I nod. The tea looks rather weak. "In a bank safe," I clarify. "I assume that the thing is now my property? Or do you want it back? You can have it back if you want."

"I heard about your problems," he says.

That's bizarre. He heard about my problems. Who did he hear that from? How are my problems making the rounds in this town? Is there an underground network of whispers and rumors that I cannot imagine to exist, but where my recent adventures are the subject of speculation?

"From whom?" I ask.

He shakes his head. "Doesn't matter. People talk about things they should keep to themselves. That's the inevitable nature of people."

I attempt to visualize a connection between him and some of the silent men who abducted me. They may all have the same background. Come to think of it, Edvardo and Michael might also share some ideological connections. In that case, I have to be careful: Edvardo could have been sent by Michael to get the diary back. However, that does not seem logical: Edvardo is on the run from people like Van Rijn, who want to misuse the diary, and Michael is the one who helps Van Rijn try to get his hands on it. So I have to rely on Edvardo. He's still my co-conspirator.

"I need to go back to London," I announce. "I can take the diary with me and deliver it to the right people over there."

"I have come to understand," he says, "that your enemies

will not let you leave Venice. Your situation is precarious; you may be arrested at any instance. I used the innocent-looking girl because you are being observed. The assumption of your enemies is that you will try to take the diary from its hiding place and then flee. Although not necessarily to London."

"I have nowhere else to go but London."

"Your situation is precarious," Edvardo repeats. "It won't improve when you arrive there. Neither will it improve when you stay here."

"What steps should I take next, in your opinion? Since I don't seem to have any options."

"The diary is less of a problem for you than your situation at home."

"Can I use it in exchange for my . . ."

He shakes his head. "Your husband does not care about the diary. He wants to take revenge on you. You want to escape that specific issue and distance yourself from him. But now, with Antonio's death, they want the blame on you; they have you in a bind."

I prefer not to discuss this aspect of my problems with him. How does he know about Antonio and the plans of my enemies? How is he so well informed about some aspects of this plot? He is a mystery, but at the same time he is particularly useful to me. Or at least I hope he is.

I want to blame Venice for my missteps, my mistakes, and my bad decisions. I am a victim of this city, which, with its effusions and atmosphere, has disturbed my common sense and well-being—and continues to do so. I can't think as clearly as before. My mind is clouded. Foggy—that would be a better term, under these circumstances.

I try to remember details of the city—and sometimes I make up details—to get that clear thinking going again. I attempt to recall the number of lions and statues I encountered here, as well as the numerous references to both open and unopened books, along with the symbolic meanings associated with them. I try to recall the wisdom of the influential thinkers and writers who visited this city. In comparison, Antonio's murder is a detail, insignificant, quickly forgotten, and hopefully forgiven. The boy was a nullity, a passerby, even a parasite. Why would anyone care about his fate, let alone the police and courts?

However, this will not be the heart of my defense before a Venetian court, a defense that I will have to conduct with the help of a translator (the language of law and justice will be too complex for me). Yes, Honorable President of this Court, I did kill the young man, but my act must be situated in the much broader and richer context of my life. Compared to that life, Antonio's life is a mere speck of dust. He is not worth the effort of this lawsuit—in fact, I have done this city a favor by removing a petty criminal, a male prostitute, a drug trafficker, from its streets.

I am convinced that the court will understand and follow this argument, logical as it is.

But, as realistic as I sometimes am, I want to avoid the risk of appearing in court at all.

Ultimately, Edvardo confronts me with a hard truth: my presence in London and my defense there are more important than the diary.

"Why are you here if you can't help me?" I ask.

"I didn't say I couldn't help you," he says, sipping his tea.

42

"How can you help me?" I ask. I wonder if he lives in this room, has found a hiding place here, or what. The place is miserable enough, and I don't see a bed. Maybe in the adjacent room. Anyway, not my problem.

"You know who I am," says Edvardo. As if that explains everything. It explains a lot, but for the sake of clarity, I want to hear him tell me again what I am to make of his reply.

"You mean: who you were in a previous life?"

"Yes."

"I know something about your past, or at least what you told me. Is it still relevant today? It places you in the ranks of Michael and Van Rijn and their accomplices."

"No," he says, empathetically, stubbornly. As if I made a serious mistake against his personal etiquette.

"No?" I repeat.

"No. Not at all. I don't belong in those ranks at all. Wasn't it clear to you that I was distancing myself from my past? I can't outrun it, unfortunately not, and it will eventually catch up with me. However, I aim to intentionally keep a safe distance from it for as long as possible. I'm no longer that man."

I wonder how that's contradictory, but let it pass. "So you are in no way an ideological ally of . . ."

He shakes his head.

There we are. A former SS officer with a problematic conscience. He probably won't be the only one. People, including those who commit crimes, are complex. And I don't know if I can link him to the worst excesses of the SS and of Nazism as a whole. I'm going to assume he was at the front and that he saw the same things I saw. What I don't know is whether he was also responsible for those crimes.

What does he propose now, based on his past experiences? Does he suggest a violent solution to my primary problem? Michael, Van Rijn, and their bodyguards are all what separates me from freedom, a situation he's aware of. Maybe all I have to do is take out the first two, and I'll be freed from my chains. It's also possible that additional players, such as the woman and others I haven't yet encountered, are involved, making the situation more complicated.

A dead Michael would pose no problem, and his disappearance would be easily explained. He has officially gone into hiding, so that charade may continue after my return to London. Van Rijn holds a subordinate position in this narrative. The bodyguards, the man in the boat? They are hired hands and will be of no consequence once their employer is out of the picture. Edvardo and I undoubtedly have enough experience together to get started with eliminating these threats. Why wouldn't we take matters into our own hands? Van Rijn and the other conspirators will certainly not hesitate to harm us. And as far as I'm concerned, I'm already wanted for murder.

But there are more people involved. At least one more: the dark woman. Haven't seen her, and I still have to understand her role in this story. For the time being, she is in the enemy camp.

"Do we have any resources?" I ask him. It appears as though he is organizing a military operation, which isn't the case.

"Money? Do you mean money?"

"That too. But . . . weapons? Wouldn't we need weapons?"

He takes a deep breath. Ten years ago, we both actively participated in a landscape that was contested by both our nations and armies, with him and I on different sides of the front. Now we serve the same masters: ourselves, first and foremost.

"What do you want to do afterwards?" I ask him, because I want to be convinced of his motives, which are still too vague for me. "What are your plans for the immediate future?"

"No more than what I wanted before," he says.

"The diary is in the hands of the right people. Nazi's exposed. The conspiracy at large made public. Fascism stopped."

"Yes, all that," he says. "And you'll be able to find the right people who can bring this about."

"We're going to hand the dairy over together, in London," I assure him. I can afford magnanimity. I can afford to make meaningless promises. He is willing to sacrifice himself for a noble cause. So much for the difference between us. I suspect he realizes that. I'm not going to ask for his deeper motives.

"You need to go back to London," he insists. "Even after we're finished here, Venice will not be a safe place for you."

"I'll take that into consideration. But I don't want Michael to return to London. Not alive, anyway."

"That much I understand. If he shows up, it will be extremely harmful to you. Are there any other problems for you concerning the lawsuit?"

I think about the man I hired. But if I believe Michael's story, that man probably left no trace and disappeared with enough money, not wanting or needing to show up again. So one less problem for me. Except when he shows up on the witness stand—a prosecution witness, as far as I'm concerned.

Here we are sitting opposite each other, Edvardo and I. Two people who don't know each other all that well and who, above all, have nothing in common. Not the culture, not the past, not the morals. Everything between us is doomed to fail. We are going to take on Michael and Van Rijn, and perhaps the anonymous dark woman too, and their entire conspiracy. We will, if necessary, tackle the whole world and, in particular, the fascist conspiracy, but we have no idea how to proceed.

Previously, I was inclined to follow the chain of events from beginning to end: Antonio, Van Rijn, and then the dark woman. Now, I want to focus on the last link in the chain: the woman herself. The house on Campo S. Angelo, with the door next to the tobacco and spirits shop and the three flats above. She lives in one of them. That much I know.

So that's where we go.

It is now afternoon. Edvardo and I are on the stakeout, somewhat hidden from sight. We don't have anything to talk about. We don't talk about our youth or our families.

The dark woman finally showing up is liberating for me.

43

She wears a flowing purple cloak (lined with what looks like white silk), over a gray dress that reaches to her knees, and elegant black shoes with mid-height heels, in keeping with the prevailing fashion. She walks decisively down the street, people get out of her way. Edvardo and I follow her without having agreed on a plan or strategy.

All this inevitably will lead to more violence and pain, but I take comfort in knowing that none of it is my fault. I didn't set this in motion. Nothing that has happened so far is more than me attempting to save my life. I readily acknowledge that I have been lying and deceiving, and I have done so as much as necessary throughout my life. I wove many webs of deceit, which I will not deny. But better alive and lying than dead after having told only the truth.

Meanwhile, the dark woman takes us through a number of narrow alleys and streets. What will we discover at the end of this walk? Van Rijn, and Michael? When they show up, what will we do? We can't rely on improvisation, although we have no fixed plan. I could do without a confrontation with any of those men right now, but I realize the choice will not be mine. I don't want to be judged for the problems I could not have avoided, and certainly not for the death of Antonio. Now, as far as my husband is concerned, I know what I will do. He will not leave Venice alive; that much is clear, improvisation or not. If Van Rijn chooses to obstruct my path, he will be reduced to mere collateral damage. He'd better not do that.

The woman has lunch in a trattoria, after which she visits a classical concert in some palace or other. We wait outside the building, assuming she will come out the same way she entered. The doorman, when asked, warns us the concert may take some time; we should not wait outside in the cold. Edvardo and I have something to eat in a pizzeria across the square, sitting at the window in silence. We have exhausted all mutual subjects.

Soon night falls again, all too fast. Finally, the dark woman emerges from the concert, along with a few hundred other smartly dressed people. She chats with some other visitors for a few moments and finally takes her leave. She continues her stroll through the city, not intending on returning to her flat yet. She enters a café and sits at the counter, chats with two women, eats a light snack, and drinks what looks like a cocktail. I wonder if she knows about our presence, about us following her, and if she is playing a game with us. She's leading us nowhere; we're just wasting our time.

"I've had enough of this wild goose chase," Edvardo comments.

"So have I," I agree. This spy thing has been a waste of time. I am cold, and even with what the near future holds in store for me, I want nothing better than to return to my warm hotel room, have a cognac and read a book, and enjoy my last moments of freedom. Without Edvardo around. However, success will not come without hardship and hard work. My freedom will be difficult to gain.

But suddenly, things change for the better, as far as we are concerned. Michael enters the cafe and approaches the woman. He leans towards her and kisses her firmly on the mouth, clearly not against her will.

There we are. Another revelation that may complicate matters.

44

"Who is *that*?" asks Edvardo. He sounds intrigued and surprised at the same time. And at a glance, he notices how surprised I am.

"That's my husband," I explain.

"Really?" He scrutinizes the couple with a frown, judging them.

"For now anyway. My husband, I mean."

"And thus he is our intended target."

"Indeed, he is."

Edvardo remains silent for a moment. In his gaze, I thought to recognize a troubled past but no repentance. I saw war in his eyes, but not peace. He probably will never know peace. I cannot, however, imagine he wore the black uniform with the silver skull and the double S. I can't believe he ever was a close ally of death and of things worse than death. However, he might have been an unwilling ally, a relatively innocent bystander in the course of historic events.

We observe the couple through the window of the bar. A group of street thugs, noisy and eager for trouble, pass by, seemingly unaware of our presence. Young men, on course for a confrontation with the rest of the world. I heard rumors and want to avoid them if at all possible. Heroin is the new king in the backstreets of Venice, as it is in London, and young lads like these either deal the stuff or are addicted to it—maybe both. Anyway, I give them a wide berth.

We keep our eyes on the bar, like we are watching a theater piece, one of those modernist, so-called humanist or nihilistic things. Maybe we've been watching nothing but a performance, an act put up solely for our own benefit. Neither of us knows what to make of this meeting, except for the fact that these two are involved in the conspiracy. My only certainty is that time is running out. And at great speed.

"I assume," Edvardo continues, "you want to act quickly now."

I nod. He is reading my mind. "That's the intention. It is certainly *my* intention. But exactly what can we do?"

I know the answer. I know very well what to do. I will do to Michael what I should have done myself two weeks ago instead of paying some idiot. Had I done that, we would not have to stare at these two lovebirds.

Then, all of a sudden, things happen. They both finish their drinks; he takes her by the arm, and together they leave the cafe quite intimately. She wraps her overcoat around her body, against the cold, and looks up for a long moment, probably at the moon.

During the night, a ghostly sun reigns over Venice: a flirtatious moon dressed in a faint wisp of mist and nothing else. This moon has witnessed the rise of the Republic and observed its heights, as well as, more recently, its decline into a tourist attraction. The moon is indifferent. That's what the woman is focusing on at the moment. And she laughs loudly when he wraps his arm around her shoulders.

The traitor.

I'm jealous because the dark woman now has Michael's undivided attention, although I would not want him back in my arms. I do not understand what is going on there because he is not interested in women and doesn't even flirt with them. Unless . . .

Unless there's a specific reason for his attention, and he needs her as part of some elaborate plan. He has the ability to be charming whenever he feels like it, and I can attest to this from personal experience. He wants something from her, which nobody else can give him. He needed me because he wanted to appear like the sort of man British society appreciated. I can't imagine how she fits in. The police will arrest me tomorrow, or the day after tomorrow. What other plot does Michael have in mind?

I'm missing something in this story. I really need to ask questions that haven't been asked before. The question I have to ask is this: who is this woman who is getting so much attention from my ex-Michael? He who is still married to me at this very moment?

"I think I know who that woman is," Edvardo says suddenly.

I confront him. Is he going to solve my puzzle? "Do you know her?"

"She looked familiar, but now I remember who she is. I recognize her from the society sections of newspapers that, you know, an intellectual is not supposed to read. That's where I have seen her before."

"An actress?"

He sneers. "Worse. The daughter of a wealthy industrialist who is mainly active in shipping and oil."

"Rich?"

"Very and even obscenely rich," Edvardo confirms.

Does that mean the man is richer than Michael? What is he doing here with a spoiled but wealthy daughter of some shipping magnate? And why does such a daughter find herself in the company of right-wing conspirators? Although this should not surprise me. Daddy, I assume, must have become rich thanks to his connections during the war and his deals with the different parties involved. Being Italian, as I assume, he will have done business with the fascists long before the conflict. He probably managed to escape any form of persecution afterwards, again thanks to his riches and connections.

And then Michael appears on the scene, chasing the daughter of the super-rich, again playing the role of the very suitable lover and husband-to-be, which means there's another reason to get rid of me. He's not interested in her body, not even in her soul. He's actually not interested in her at all, as he was never interested in me. We—myself, the dark woman and probably a string of women I know nothing about—are only means to a specific end, as we have been all through his life.

I stand in his way. I stand in the way of his renewed conquest of riches greater than his own.

45

We now follow Michael and the dark beauty northwest, toward my own hotel, all the way to the canal. They enter another hotel, the Grand Canal, not too far from where I am staying. It appears that our tastes align, despite his hotel being slightly less impressive than mine. But probably just as expensive. And they go in together. Do they share a room? What exactly is their game, and more precisely, his?

Edvardo and I hesitate. We are standing a hundred meters from the hotel, with our backs to the canal where a loud, puffing, and smelly vaporetto passes, with a group of cheering schoolgirls on board. Should we enter the hotel and find out more about the two lovebirds? That could potentially escalate the situation and likely resolve only a few of the issues. Michael might recognize me if they both continue to hang out in the lobby. Edvardo, on the other hand, is a stranger to Michael.

All this is beginning to look like a spy movie. Edvardo, with his dark overcoat and hat, could pass for an ominous British secret agent. This doesn't even require much imagination. Or (more appropriately) a former Nazi in the service of, say, the Americans. They are all too willing to depend on their former adversaries in certain clear-cut professional roles. In this particular scenario, who am I? The archetypal and inevitable femme fatale? Who would rather use poison than a knife? Poison. Now there's an idea. I need to contemplate the possibility of using poison to eliminate Michael.

"I'll go inside for a moment and look around," he suggests. "Will you wait here?"

I'm not going anywhere, not in the immediate future. He walks decisively to the hotel, as if he belongs there. As devious as he is, he probably will find out a few things about the guests staying there.

So I wait, strolling back and forth, impatient. The neighborhood is lively with tourists, not deterred by the damp chill. They dress warmly, with fur coats for the ladies and large woolen overcoats for the men. Everyone of rank wears a hat. Despite my somewhat outlandish attire, I generally receive no attention.

It takes no more than ten minutes before Edvardo shows up again. He joins me; we take shelter in shadows. "Your husband and the woman, who is registered as his wife, have been sharing a room for two days," he says. "They rented that room for an indefinite period of time. They are nowhere to be seen at the moment, but I assume they are still at the hotel. This is the only exit for guests."

I could get Michael caught in bed with another woman if I could organize a notary, the police, or someone official. A woman, this time, but still more proof of his infidelity. Just one more argument with which Master Morse can turn any court case in my favor.

But I need to find a more decisive and definitive solution and stop mucking around. A charge of infidelity will not deter Michael. We're playing this game at a very different level now. I am, and he certainly is. The woman, on the other hand, is negligible. She is part of a conspiracy somewhere, but she has now become of secondary importance. Edvardo can do whatever he wants with the German diary. What I want is Michael's head on a stake, nothing less than that. Figuratively, of course.

Am I going to do that myself? The head on a stake? I'll have to think about it for a moment and about how this should be done. We are talking about murder, no less. If his body is found here in Venice, there might be a problem—one that probably will reflect on my court case. Officially, he is somewhere in the home country, still in hiding. He shouldn't be in Venice at all. I suspect he has been traveling under a false name and with an equally false passport. In that case, he plays right into my hands, because I want to see him disappear in a most definitive way. Even if his body turns up here, his identity will remain a mystery, as I will take steps to prevent identification.

I heard corpses showing up in the lagoon once in a while. Suicide, mainly. Not an epidemic, but the occasional anonymous body finds itself in the mortuary, with the police unable to identify the victim. Nobody will connect the body to Michael, who is believed to have vanished in London.

He must be dealt with. For good. One way or the other, but without me being involved in any respect.

I explain this to Edvardo, whom I cannot but trust. He nods thoughtfully and looks at me seriously, as if murder is a subject worth considering between us. Perhaps he sympathizes with me because I've put myself in this uncomfortable situation and am left with only one possible solution. It's a course of action that even he might come to regret. Or not, as he remains somewhat of a mystery to me.

"Can you help me with this plan, Edvardo?" I ask him explicitly. And I'm sure he understands what I'm demanding of him.

"These people are not my enemies," he explains, carefully choosing his words. "That husband of yours, and the woman."

"They are dealing with the people who threatened you and who tried to get their hands on the diary." Do I need to explain he finds himself in a position somewhat similar to mine?

"That's right, yes," he admits. "But not your husband or that woman."

I understand what he means. Michael is not directly his problem. Michael is no obstacle for him.

But I can't afford to be understanding. I don't want to hesitate or delay, either. I have little time left.

"They are part of that conspiracy at large," I insist. "And I ask you as a friend, Edvardo, to help me out here. Then, when my problem is resolved, we will deliver the diary to the appropriate people back in London."

I don't need to remind him that the diary is still in my safe.

And so he's going to do the deed. Let's put it plainly: he intends to murder Michael and dispose of the body. My price for the diary.

"Perhaps the solution you propose is a bit too radical," he suggests. Although he does not seem to shy away from murder.

Smart, isn't he? He at once knows how the cards are stacked. This means that he also clearly understands his own position.

"I take responsibility for the further consequences of my solution," I assure him. If things go wrong, I want to be far away from Venice—that's what I actually mean.

"It is and remains a moral issue," he says, looking at the hotel.

Morality? Is he, of all people, engaging in a debate about morality? He who once donned the black uniform? Did he not, barely ten years ago, march behind those terrible banners and effortlessly raised his right arm when his leader appeared on the balcony? What did he actually do during the war?

And now he's going to stand here and whine that the fate I reserve for Michael is a bit too radical?

I count on him to carry out my plan, with or without his reservations. But what is the most suitable plan? I must take into account that, in the worst-case scenario, the link between a corpse in the lagoon and Michael will still be made. I must not underestimate the determination or resourcefulness of the local police. Despite the false documents found on the body (or the complete lack of documents), someone might make a connection between the corpse and the missing Michael.

I prefer not to take any risks. So I need an alibi, just in case. This suggests that I surround myself with individuals who are familiar to me, while Edvardo handles the dirty work. I must make sure I have a verifiable alibi. The issue is that I don't know anyone who can provide me with such an alibi.

Or do I?

Well, I know someone who can provide a very decent alibi, while Edvardo sends Michael off to the eternal hunting grounds. He will make sure that the time of Michael's death can be confirmed, for example, because his watch has stopped. Yes, I got that from one of those detective books. And in the meantime, I can prove that I have been elsewhere. I know someone who can give me a perfect alibi.

This is how we're going to do it.

46

The next morning, immediately after a sufficiently extensive breakfast, providing sufficient energy for half a day, I ask reception for the telephone number of the Questura and contact Inspector Martinengo, the only virtuous man in this city. At least the only virtuous man I know of.

He's clearly a bit disturbed by my call. He doesn't expect to hear from me. Why would I call him? The British are not explicitly requesting my extradition. He himself will not take me handcuffed to the airport and push me onto a plane to London. I hope he doesn't associate me with Antonio's murder, a case that could potentially fall under a colleague's investigation instead of his own.

"What exactly can I do for you, Signora?" he asks politely.

You can provide me with that airtight alibi for the moment my husband is murdered here in Venice. That is what I finally agreed with Edvardo (who is still reluctant). My motto was to be fast, efficient, and definitive. Edvardo would adhere to that. If the body is found, which is very unlikely, the time of death will appear to be this morning, exactly when I'm having my talk with my favorite inspector. The police themselves provide the best alibi.

By the way, am I capable of murder? Really? A lady of my class? Even if I had a good reason, I wouldn't kill my husband for his fortune, because I completely trust the British judicial process, and it will rule in my favor. The money is already within my reach. But that was before Michael turned up and set his own destructive plans into motion. Before he became a real menace.

"I want to meet you this morning, inspector," I say, "because I want to talk to you about my further stay here."

"That stay depends entirely on you, Signora. I told you so before: I cannot force you to return to London. You go, or you don't go. The whole thing is not our problem. The police in London have not contacted us again. Not yet. What will we have a conversation about then?"

I had misjudged our lack of subject matter. My mistake, completely. He doesn't need to see me, and my alibi falls apart. That is not such a favorable evolution.

Unless I think of something else.

"I'm being shadowed, Inspector. Unknown men constantly follow me. Could those be your officers?"

"No, ma'am. We don't shadow you. Why should we?" He sounds vaguely indignant.

"Maybe I should file a complaint, don't you think?"

He sighs. My stubborn lack of logic bothers him. "Who do you want to file a complaint against?"

"Against persons unknown, if necessary. But I think I know who those men are."

"Then who are they?" He still doesn't sound really interested.

"They are paid by the family of my husband, Inspector. That much I think I know with great certainty. I don't know what they're planning. Maybe they want to kidnap me or something, and take me back to London against my will."

"You have too much imagination," he says. "That's not how it works in real life."

No, this is not how things operate in the land of the mafia. Nobody here has ever resorted to such practices. Who does he think he is fooling?

"You are unfamiliar with the tenacity of certain British families," I inform him, "who will stop at nothing to avoid sharing their fortune with others. With me, in particular. Maybe they want to kill me. Then they can definitively resolve the issue."

I hear him sigh again. It sounds melodramatic, I know. The story suits Venice, but still . . . Isn't this the city where Casanova felt at home—that boastful and deceptive charmer? Isn't this the city of masks and carnivals? Of appearances and deception? Where intrigue and murder are the common tools of criminals and the elite?

"All right, come over, Signora," he finally says. "It's probably useless, this whole thing, but I'll file a report, and I'll gather some information through my network. Could those men be British private investigators?"

"They would rather be the kind of men who are not averse to doing dangerous jobs, as long as they are paid well for it. We too face the issue of organized crime, Inspector. But you're right, I'll pass by your office."

For that I have to take a taxi across the water, which turns out to be incredibly expensive for a trip of no more than fifteen minutes, but there are too many detours on foot. Standing on this threshold, I will soon acquire a fortune. So what does it matter?

I look at my watch. I have not arranged a precise timetable with Edvardo, but we have agreed that he will carry out his assignment this morning. So when I am dropped off at a quay a little later, minus a few banknotes, I am convinced that our plan still holds water. I'm working diligently on my alibi.

The Questura, which I walk towards, is an austere building, as old as the rest of the city. Maybe it was once a prison. There are certainly plenty of bars on the windows. Inside, I am led to Inspector Martinengo's office, on the first floor. The office is situated at the rear of the building, offering an unimpressive view of roofs and sparse brick walls. He must have become accustomed to the surroundings by now. With a gesture, he invites me to sit down. "Signora Barth," he says, without much enthusiasm. "You are causing us extra work. Anyway, I will listen to you. Are you truly certain that someone is following you?"

"Absolutely, Inspector. Maybe not all the time, but often enough to worry me."

"By?"

"Two men. Maybe more. One is bald. The other looks too mundane to describe."

Nevertheless, he writes down a few things in a notebook. With a pencil. And he frowns. Is this case suddenly interesting now? "How are they dressed? Expensive, common, foreign?"

"Dark overcoat, hat, and black shoes. All of good quality, it seems to me. At least they're not the scruffy types one sees around here so often."

"You don't give me many useful details, unless you want me to question half of the foreign visitors to this city."

"Both are big. Bigger than the average Italian. That is why I am convinced that they are foreigners."

"British, I may assume. Considering your background . . ."

"You are probably right." He writes down everything without further criticism. These details will go into his report later, along with the time of this conversation.

"And with this virtually meaningless description, you come here, insisting on seeing me, while you know I cannot do anything. You must be aware of that, must you not?"

I can tell him that he is my favorite Venetian policeman. But that's not going to help my case.

"Why can't you do something?" I ask. I try to sound innocent and naive. I'm trying my best. As if the whole world is morally obliged to do something when I complain about a nuisance.

"Do you believe that we have the resources available to personally protect you? We don't have that, I'm afraid. When a prominent politician arrives on an official visit, for example, Rome will send us extra officers and perhaps agents of State Security. But you are an ordinary citizen."

"An ordinary *foreign* citizen," I insist.

"Still without any special status. There is no reason for me to believe you are in danger. The only advice I can give you is this: go back to London. The police can do more for you there than we can. Do you still have business here to take care of?"

Now I have to be careful. I don't want him to think about any pressing matter that requires my attention here. "No," I say. "I'm here as a tourist. But that doesn't mean . . ."

"No, no," he quickly interrupts. "Everyone should feel safe, especially tourists. Please stay on the busier streets, Signora. And don't walk around at night in neighborhoods where you don't belong. Venice is a safe city, but inevitably there is the occasional crime. This is Italy, after all—still a country that has not left the misery of the war behind. These tourists, like yourself, might be naive enough to believe that everyone is appreciative of their presence here. And that they can flaunt their wealth with impunity. That's a dangerous assumption." He looks as if he disapproves of that wealth.

"I'll be careful, inspector."

His gaze glides over my clothes for a moment. He may be drawing the wrong conclusions. He can't know whether my less than conventional clothes are not the new fashion in Paris and therefore an affront to local petty crime.

"I will request additional patrols, particularly in the vicinity of the luxury hotels, Signora. We can't do more, I'm afraid. Not without any specific indications of a crime in progress."

When the young officer I met earlier in his company opens the door to his office, he glances up. The officer speaks quickly to the inspector. Martinengo asks a question, gets an answer, and then barks an order.

"I'm sorry, Signora," he says to me, "but an urgent matter requires my full attention. I have to end this conversation."

I get up. He accompanies me into the hallway. At the end of it, four men are waiting for him, two of them in uniform. They all look at the inspector at the same time. He says to me, "I'm counting on you to find the exit on your own, right?"

And he quickly joins the four men.

Something is going on in the safe city of Venice.

47

I return to the hotel, on foot this time. I watch out for the ever-damp cobblestones—enemies of my shoes and my balance. I regularly look behind me. I have talked myself into a state of paranoia. However, it doesn't appear that anyone is following me. Plenty of faces and shadows though; no shortage of them. People who peer out of windows or from behind display cases in shops and who judge me interesting enough to stop what they are doing for a moment. However, it does not seem like a systematic observation. The paranoia may be unfounded.

At the hotel, I return at once to my room and wait. I have agreed with Edvardo that he will not contact me here but that we will meet at seven o'clock in a bar nearby. I have to exercise patience and caution. Most of all, caution.

I exercise patience. I try to read my book, my fingers clutched across its spine, but after a while I give up. None of it gets through to me—not a sentence, not a thought. The writer will hate me for this. There is an Italian newspaper next to me, a few days old, that I want to read. But my patience doesn't extend that far either. Perhaps I should live a small, narrow, and modest life, away from the temptations of this age. Live on my own, with almost no contact with the outside world.

Now that I'm thinking this over, I realize Martinengo made no move to arrest me, so there's no suspicion on his part concerning Antonio.

Two or three hours slowly drag by. I'm considering writing a letter to Master Morse, but that letter would take a few days to reach London. So I better send a telegram, although I wouldn't know what I have to share with him. I've been here for over a week now, and I don't want to leave right away. Although I would be better off taking a night train to somewhere else, where I will no longer be confronted with my problems.

No, this is not going to work either. When Edvardo has done his job properly, my problems will be as good as solved. So just be patient. Just a little while longer now.

Hunger overwhelms me again. But it's almost seven o'clock, and I have to see Edvardo. I change into civilized camouflage, a neutral overcoat, and a scarf to maintain my anonymity, then walk to the bar located a few streets away from the hotel. It's still quiet there. The bar appears to be primarily frequented by tourists, with some even having cocktails. It's five to seven. Edvardo isn't here yet. I sit at a table in the back and wait, enjoying a cup of coffee. I wait. Half an hour, an hour. I'll forfeit a portion of my night's sleep for another cup of coffee. Edvardo doesn't show up. Something's wrong. I consider him a punctual person, someone who keeps his appointments. Someone who knows how to reach me when plans change.

After an hour and a half, I walk back to the hotel. I am worried. This little caper of ours does not go as planned. What's my next step? How can I contact Edvardo? How do I find him again? Where did he go? What went wrong? What should I do now?

If I knew the answers to those questions, I would take action immediately. But I don't know anything.

Close to the hotel, I realize that I haven't eaten yet. I don't feel hungry, but I need to provide my body with energy, so I duck into a trattoria and quickly consume some pasta and a glass of red wine to counteract the caffeine.

At the reception, I ask if there is a message for me, but there is not. Edvardo may have run into trouble, maybe had problems disposing of the body. He may have needed to bribe some public servants or police officials to get him out of trouble—something I would not put past him. However, he doesn't appear to have any updates for me.

I retreat to the bar with a boring club soda, the only drink I trust at the moment. This place lacks inspiration, primarily due to the mirrored panels adorning three of the walls. Four men disguised as businessmen hang at the bar. None of them wears a tie. They cast but a fleeting glance at me.

My strategy? What about it? Do I call inspector Martinengo on some flimsy pretext and inquire about incidents in the city? What kinds of incidents? Something involving a man matching Edvardo's description of having been caught in some suspicious act? The inspector will find my interest intriguing and my story implausible. What exactly do I want to know, and whom am I talking about? Is there something going on he should know about? Is there something going on that falls within the inspector's field of authority?

Therefore, I won't be contacting the inspector. It wouldn't be a wise decision. But then again, if I don't, I limit my sources of information.

To zero.

What could have happened? Why didn't Edvardo meet me?

Did something serious happen to him? Are our plans collapsing on themselves?

The answer emerges almost instantly and comes as no surprise. It is Michael who leisurely walks into the bar, as if nothing is forcing him and nothing is going wrong, at least not for him. He acts like a tourist or a businessman enjoying a night off after closing a very profitable deal. He just knows that I will be here. He at once and without hesitation walks over to me, sits down opposite me at the table, examines my non-alcoholic drink with interest, doesn't even frown, but says, "You know why I'm here, Ellen."

It's not a question; it's an observation. He knows that, because of his appearance, I realize the trouble I have gotten into. Because he's here, and he's still alive, and that can only mean . . .

"You don't seem to want to learn the lesson, Ellen," he continues.

I glance at him, but I keep my mouth shut. That seems the best strategy for the time being.

"And by that I mean," he continues, "as I told you before, you have to solve your own problems, do the dirty work yourself, and so on. Didn't I tell you so? Do you recall what happened in London when you sent that man after me? That was when things started to take a wrong turn for you. And now you let it happen again, Ellen. It's becoming tedious. Same scenario, same outcome. You just don't learn. It seems as though you are unwilling to learn from experience. I thought better of you."

I still don't say anything. But I'm sinking deeper and deeper, metaphysically speaking.

"What were you actually thinking? Did you truly believe that you could send that shady Nazi mercenary after me, assuming he too would outsmart me? You've seen what kind of bodyguards I have, right? And then you also underestimate me personally. Foolish of you, Ellen. You will never become the queen of crime you think you are."

"Where is he?"

"Your mercenary? No idea. I have people who take care of that sort of thing. I myself don't bother. His fate shouldn't concern you either. He's gone from your life; that's all you need to know. I'm still here, where I'm supposed to be. Here, in Venice. And you, Ellen? Are you where you should be? Obviously not. You don't belong here at all. You don't understand this city; you don't understand London either, and what you certainly don't understand is how people like me, with my background, think—and live. And how we shall always be able to survive. Against—I might say—many odds."

"You needed me to be presentable for people like yourself, Michael. You were not at all interested in who I was. You needed a woman as a sort of alibi. You needed a show wedding; you needed a front for the things you were doing behind everybody's back. You never intended for me to discover the truth, nor for me to pursue my own life. Well, that went wrong, didn't it?"

He nods. "I admit this may have been a miscalculation on my part. I may have underestimated your vigor and your resolve. However, things happened as they happened; here we are, and new times are dawning. Times when people are becoming much more open-minded. Even on account of men like me. Within a few years, no one will care that I like other men or have sex with them. In a few years, it won't even be considered a crime."

"All the better," I say. "All the better for everyone involved. But you're not going to the scaffold because you're gay, Michael."

"No? Why then?"

"Because you committed a murder."

His face lights up. "Ah! You're wrong again. Once again, you fail to understand who I am. I didn't commit murder. No one will be able to link me to any murder, either here or in London. I am careful. You, on the other hand . . ."

Yes, I already know it all. The police can link me to a murder and perhaps also to a conspiracy to commit a second murder.

If anyone goes to the scaffold, it's me. But we're not there yet. There is still a long way to go before I reach the steps of the scaffold.

Although, as things stand now, the situation is looking bad as far as I'm concerned. Here in Venice, I am confronted with people whose plans and needs are not in my favor.

"First and foremost, I want you to get me that diary," he continues. "It's rubbish; I don't care, but my friends want to get their hands on it. I would like to give them that pleasure."

"And next?"

"The police will be arresting you for the murder of Antonio. If you are nice and waive your claims to my assets—and those of my family—we will provide you with the best lawyer available, and we will ensure the investigation is not conducted too thoroughly and that there will be sufficient reason to doubt your involvement in both murders here. Money can do wonders in this country. Best-case scenario: you get off without going to jail. And we forget the rest too—these problems you caused us. I have my British lawyer draft some documents for you to sign, after which our mutual problems will be resolved. You can't go back to England, that's for sure. It's best to avoid going back there because you won't have any friends left anymore. But hey, Venice is quite nice, and I know you have money of your own, and you can keep what you have on your account, even if most of it comes from me."

"How generous," I say.

"Right? No more luxury hotels, I'm afraid, but you will survive. And you can go back to work. Who knows, your old job? No, not a journalist, but that other job. A tall, beautiful, blonde woman in this part of Italy? You'll make a killing, even at your age."

48

That's exactly what my terribly conniving husband has in store for me: he reduces me to what he believes I should be: a whore. And, to make things worse, he then makes a snide remark about my age. Well, that's clear enough. All my efforts to be anything like a meaningful wife to him are now thrown unto the trash heap. Oh, they can call me an *escort*, or whatever, if they want to be polite and personable. There are a few obfuscating terms that help disguise the reality, and *escort* is of course just one of them. But nevertheless, this is what I am in his eyes and always will be.

A *whore*.

I don't have any personal shame about being a whore, as I voluntarily chose that life. With the utmost dignity I could afford, I practiced that profession as honorably and safely as possible. I strolled from appointment to appointment, dressed in silk and perfume. I don't despise the girls, women, and even older women who must navigate the streets, alleyways, and passers-by, only to find themselves standing on a filthy street corner, regardless of the circumstances. I don't look down on them. They deserve a better life because they risk it all again and again, and why? They occupy a social role that other women, particularly those of the citizen class, find objectionable. My sympathy goes to the whores.

My sympathy does not extend to their customers.

But I also knew another life. I'm not referring to the world in which Michael once belonged and continues to belong. No. Not the world of upstarts who exercise power over everyone thanks to their money. Those who fold and bend the world as they see fit. The very rich upstarts who don't contribute to society because they do anything to not pay taxes (and get away with it), who make money from wars if not from worse. Those people. The *Michaels*.

I knew a different life: during and after the war, as a woman who made choices for herself, who was in danger when she wanted to, who was considered their equal by brave, hard men at the front, who with a pen and typewriter was going to tackle the world. I have known that life.

At a certain point, I folded. Michael. The temptation of riches. The other life. The sort of life that soars miles above the mundane world. It turned out to be a mistake, but I have the right to make mistakes in my life. Even sizable ones.

Indeed, this moment now feels like a liberating experience. This moment. Michael telling me that I have to work as a whore again. Yes, actually, it is liberating. Because he cuts me out of his life and anything associated with it. All the lies and pretenses. He doesn't realize it, but it's liberating, and he's actually doing me a favor. Yes, I still have some money left, some of which is mine, and some of which he has given me over the past two years out of pure selfish calculation. And I keep that money. It's not a fortune; it won't last me a lifetime, but I can start something for myself. Not in prostitution, however.

However, I might consider returning to my other previous job.

Newspapers are everywhere. They must be filled with stories, and preferably with The Truth. Not very many people can write good stories. Few are motivated enough to dig out the truth.

At the very least, I hope Michael allows me to leave. Because I still know too much about him. About his friends. All kinds of dark but harmful secrets—I know them.

However, I am not grateful to him. Not really. He is the product of a world that needs to disappear quickly. He is a man without any morals or emotions. He lives in a machine and thinks he is the operator. But that world does not disappear. That world dominates life more and more, increases the pressure on all of us, and crushes any opposition. We have fought wars, not to be free but, on the contrary, to be even more chained by those who promise us dignity. They promise us dignity, but they want our souls.

We're still in the hotel bar, Michael and I. He holds the best cards; I hold the rubbish. He has outlined clearly enough what is going to happen. The logical course of events. He comes out of this virtually unscathed, even richer than he was before, with no one to stand in his way anymore. There are the people he hangs out with who—in my opinion at least—are completely unreliable, but that won't be his problem. I have tasted wealth for several years (his wealth, yes, I admit), and now I return to what I was, not entirely impecunious. After perhaps spending some time in a Venetian cell, I will be free again.

It doesn't seem like such a bad exchange. It doesn't seem like such a negative proposal at all.

However, there is a downside. Unfortunately, there is a downside.

Some people have died. Antonio and now Edvardo as well. None of them were innocent. None of them were just casual bystanders.

And still . . .

I don't want to spend a minute in a Venetian cell.

I want a lot of other things, but they are out of my reach now.

I will have to make choices. There are few things left to save.

So I take Michael to the bank, where I rent a safe. A beautiful building, this bank, as those institutions always are. Enough copper and marble and statues to fill three palaces. Old-fashioned welcome for customers like me, polite but also condescending, while the mob and the lower middle class are kept out by a burly doorman. You don't just become a customer here, not without the necessary references. In my case, my account at Lloyds. Michael himself is also allowed inside, into the reception area at least, where two gentlemen in their forties are patiently waiting for customers. Both speak passable English, but they object to Michael's presence. No, the vault is off limits to him. This is only accessible to customers. The gentleman is not a customer, so . . .

Michael looks disturbed, but nothing can be done about the situation. "I'll wait here for you," he says, and takes a seat in the foyer, under the watchful eyes of the two men, while I am expertly and silently guided downstairs by a third man who suddenly appeared out of nowhere. The entire building has no smell—literally none, which is amazing in this city. Not that it stinks or anything (except sometimes for the canals and alleys), but there is always a smell of human activity and of a long, deep, and above all, musty history. Not here.

The attendant checks my ticket, compares the number with my safe, examines his book of registered owners, glances at my passport, and then leaves me alone. I open the safe, slide out the steel box, and open it.

On top of the folder with the diary lies a gun.

I recognize the weapon immediately. It's a Luger P08 pistol. Anyone who fought on the front against the Nazis knows this kind of weapon. It was feverishly sought after by the Allied soldiers, who were all too happy to relieve fallen Germans of it. There are still thousands of copies of that pistol circulating, especially because it has been around since the beginning of the century or so.

This weapon is special because it bears the double silver lightning of the SS.

It's not my weapon. I don't have a gun. Definitely not a Luger P08. I only used this safe once to deposit the diary. I haven't been here since. Someone else gained access to it and left the gun behind. For me. Especially for me, in case I needed a gun.

There is only one person who can do that. Who, I assume, rented a safe in this institution so that he could be alone down here, and who then managed to get my safe open. Which, I assume, is not evident.

I pick up the gun and slide the magazine out. It's fully loaded. I push the magazine back in place, click off the safety, and load a round. The weapon functions flawlessly, looking as pristine as new due to its meticulous maintenance. There's only just one person who would own such a weapon and take care of it.

Who wants to help me, as it were, from beyond the grave. A man who is more of a mystery than I realized. And who will now remain a mystery.

I switch the safety back on and slip the gun into the pocket of my overcoat. Then I take the diary out of the box, push the box back into the safe, and close it again.

Michael is waiting for me upstairs.

A surprise awaits him. But not now.

I nod at him, and without waiting for him, I walk outside into the street. I need fresh air.

He follows.

<h1 style="text-align:center">49</h1>

The plot now becomes complicated, treacherously complicated even, but at the same time it also unravels itself as a possible solution to my problems. I possess at least one advantage, albeit not the one I desired, as none of the people involved in this plot know about the gun. I may not solve its riddle, but I do not regret having it.

After a long walk, we arrive at Campo S. Angelo again—the house with the tobacconist on the ground floor—where the rich, dark-haired woman lives or at least has a residence, which in itself sounds like part of a conspiracy.

Michael ascends the stairs. I follow faithfully. He knocks on the top-floor door and, without waiting for an answer, opens it and we enter a somewhat neglected but (at first glance) clean apartment. The woman gets up from an armchair by the window, puts a book on a side table, looks at Michael, then looks at me, and asks a question in a language I don't recognize. He gives a short answer in a neutral tone.

"You have the diary?" she asks me in English. Her accent is pleasant; she knows the language well but doesn't speak it often enough.

I hold out the cardboard folder to her. She opens it, looks at the contents, closes the folder again, and places it on top of the book on the table. Then she asks Michael another question. She probably wants to know what will happen to me now. Michael shakes his head and answers. I vaguely recognize some words, but not their context, leaving me uncertain about the direction of their conversation. What are they actually speaking? Spanish? Or an Italian dialect? Probably the latter. But where does Michael get his knowledge of that language?

They're talking about my fate, that's for sure.

The gun weighs heavily in my jacket pocket. They must have noticed it, right? No, apparently not. None of them expects me to be armed. They don't judge me as dangerous. Ah, a capital mistake.

The woman steps across the room to a dresser, picks up the receiver of a black ebonite telephone, dials a four-digit number, and waits. A voice comes over the receiver, and a brief conversation develops. About me. Of course they're talking about me. Decisions have to be made. The woman is getting her instructions, I assume. She ends the call and speaks to Michael.

"We'll wait a minute," Michael says to me. "Sit down. Coffee?"

"No, thank you," I say. "I don't want to wait. I did what you wanted me to do. The matter must be settled now. I don't want to go to court. I don't want to go to jail, not even for one day."

"We can arrange these things," he says. He and the woman sit down. I take a seat in an armchair. It is covered with red velvet. Some effort has been made in the decoration of this otherwise unremarkable apartment.

They won't let me go. That much is clear to me now. Their plan does not include my survival. And so something has to be done. Like, I pull out the gun, threaten them, and run, and that's the last I hear from them. But I want to know what else they plan to do. I am interested in learning about their future plans concerning this story. Maybe everything will turn out fine. So for now I'm not doing anything.

Fifteen minutes later, I hear steps on the stairs. Van Rijn and one of the men who accompanied him earlier enter the apartment, which is suddenly very small and cramped. Van Rijn looks at me, but I see no recognizable expression in his gaze. I'm just part of the story. A word in a sentence from that story, a sentence someone said a long time ago, that's all I am. Where does that story stand now? Michael assists Van Rijn and his clients, who are determined to obtain the diary at any cost. Van Rijn assists Michael in resolving his personal issue, which involves me. My unfortunate person, reduced to a problem.

Van Rijn now has the diary. He speaks to the woman in their common language. The woman gets up and puts on her cloak. She says something to Van Rijn and then to Michael. He suddenly looks shocked, responds, but finds it difficult to get his words out. He clearly didn't anticipate what is about to happen. She snaps something at him—just two sentences, but they clearly change his life. He has turned pale. Things are not going his way, that's for sure.

I dare to guess what's going on. He thought he had seduced her, the rich heiress, with the intention of adding even more substance to his own fortune. A man like him can never have too much money. But she now tells him that she is only here for the diary and to please certain other people. She doesn't want anything to do with him anymore. That's my conclusion, and to be honest, I secretly take pleasure in this outcome. This is the fate he deserves.

Michael wants to keep her from leaving, but the anonymous young man steps between the two of them, between Michael and the woman. She at once exits the apartment. Van Rijn looks at Michael for a moment, says something, and gestures for me to go outside as well.

I've barely made it into the hallway outside the apartment when a shot rings out. And then one more. I turn around, wanting to go back for whatever stupid reason, but the young man comes out. He's empty-handed, and I assume he left the gun behind. He looks at Van Rijn. He utters the word "Dead," which may be the only English word he knows. With a gesture of his head, Van Rijn forces me outside.

The woman is nowhere to be seen. Van Rijn and the young man guide me into the street. No one appears to be alarmed by the shots, likely due to their relatively low volume.

I suspect these will be my last moments in Venice. If Van Rijn has his way, they definitely will. And it depends on him. He just settled the score with Michael. I'm the other problematic witness. They could have done it in there, too.

I have other plans, which directly cross their own. I want to survive.

"The police," Van Rijn tells me, "have found a body in a canal. They don't like this one bit: a corpse ruining the view of their city. It's detrimental for tourism. You can imagine what impression that leaves on visitors. Of course they will make that body disappear quickly. It carried documents indicating it was your friend Edvardo, or at least the man you knew by that name. He will have his funeral, but no one will attend. Certainly not you. It's unfortunate, but there's nothing you can do about the situation anymore. As for your husband, he too will be identified. Another mysterious death for the police. They're going to have to work overtime."

"What happens now?" I am thinking about Inspector Martinengo, who will be given the responsibility for both bodies. He will probably never know the truth. How far away is he from retirement? He deserves the quieter life he is undoubtedly looking forward to. He will soon be freed from me too; that much is clear.

"With you? We could conclude the affair as your husband suggested. But we don't like his plan. Keep you alive? No, that is an unthinkable risk. The diary is worth much more than you realize. It has a special value for the people who pay us. They don't want to leave any traces, and certainly no witnesses. They don't want to do anything that puts them at risk."

We reach a quay, where a motorboat is waiting for us. It is a beautiful boat with a deck of carefully waxed teak, dark red leather interior upholstery, and a red-white pennant on the short mast with the navigation light. It's possible that the man operating the boat is the same one from the previous trip. Are they taking me back to that house? Will my execution take place there, and will my corpse subsequently vanish into the lagoon? Will I ever be found?

Will Martinengo have to add a third corpse to his list?

"So I also show up in a canal or something?"

"We're still considering the options," Van Rijn says. We're sitting on the bench in the cabin. The motorboat pushes off and slowly moves past palazzos and groups of tourists. I pull my coat tight around me and stick both hands in my pockets. The interior of the boat is chilly. What do they actually have to consider? A suitable place to dump my body?

"I personally regret this state of affairs," says Van Rijn. "I like you, Signora Barth. You are an independent woman, enterprising, and intelligent. There are organizations like ours that could use someone like you. I sincerely mean that. But I only act on instructions, and those instructions are given by people who do not know you and who have therefore not learned to appreciate your qualities."

"That's a shame," I say. I remain calm, even now, when my life is at stake. Only if I stay calm can I save it.

"Indeed," he agrees. He looks outside, at the canal. The young man next to him has also diverted his attention slightly. I can act now, but we are still in Venice on the Grand Canal, where there are too many onlookers. I want to act, but somewhere further away from civilization.

Van Rijn has fallen silent. What is he thinking about? Oh well, not my problem. I have no need to get to know him better. I don't want to know where he comes from or what sort of life he leads. It will be of no concern to me. He will arrange for me to be deposed of by his anonymous executioners. They clearly want to be civilized about it, so I assume they will do it painlessly. As far as I'm concerned, I'm not in favor of all that civilized violence. There is no worse ideology than the one that coats the most abject crimes with a patina of reason. We have had enough experience with that throughout this century.

We leave the canal and move into open water, towards a narrow strip of land. There are no buildings, people, or boats in sight.

"I'm sorry too, Van Rijn," I say. "Really."

He at once notices that this is not just a casual comment. I speak with a conviction not to be expected from a willing victim. He realizes something is wrong and turns his head towards me. But he doesn't make it all the way. Too slow. He sits two meters away from me, no more, and a British officer taught me how to shoot at longer range, even with a pistol. Two meters is easy.

I only need one bullet for him, which literally goes straight through his head, and its fragments reach the other side of his skull, leaving a big hole. That bullet, or what's left of it, also shatters the window behind Van Rijn. Who is now no longer Van Rijn but a corpse that slides off the couch.

Before the former Van Rijn hits the floor, I shoot a second time. Once you start, it's difficult to stop. I also have the advantage of surprise, and I want to keep it that way. I aim at the pilot. He's four meters away from me, but I don't miss either. The boat continues to move on, no problem, but there is no one at the wheel anymore.

The young man in the dark overcoat stares at me. I see no calculation in his gaze, only fear. That tells me enough. Either he is not armed, or he has no intention of drawing his weapon because he has seen how very fast I am with mine.

I count on him to have a strong drive for life. Or that he's just scared.

"Gun?" I ask him. In English.

He understands me and shakes his head.

"*Togliti il cappotto,*" I tell him.

He carefully and slowly takes off his coat and drops it on the cabin floor. As far as I can see, he isn't carrying a weapon. "*Lei parla inglese?*"

He nods. "Take me back to land," I tell him. "Near the Carlton Hotel. Then you sail away again. I don't want to see you around, understand? How you explain all this to your boss is your business. Two dead. They will certainly understand how serious I am. That I just won't let myself be messed with. As far as I'm concerned, this can end here; but if necessary, I'll cause even more damage. Do you understand what I'm saying?"

"*Si, Signora,*" he says. I doubt it, but the message will be clear. He crawls up to the pilot, whom he drags from his seat without any consideration for the body. The proximity of death does not seem to bother him. I wonder if he was once a soldier and experienced war. No, he's too young for the latter. I reach into the pockets of his overcoat but find no weapon.

He takes control of the boat and makes a wide turn. I stand

next to him and look at the instruments in the cabin. The boat doesn't have a radio, so the young man can't warn anyone.

He slowly steers back into the canal. He wisely stays clear of other vessels. He keeps his gaze focused on the water and the immediate surroundings. Not another word is exchanged between us. That won't be necessary either.

A little later I get off at the quay at the hotel, with the Luger back in the pocket of my overcoat. The young man immediately sails away, probably worried that someone will notice the two bodies and the damage to the boat. I rush into the hotel. I estimate that it will take me at most fifteen minutes to pack my things. I don't have to worry about checking out. Long before anyone comes after me, I'm on my way to Rome or wherever.

But then I hesitate. I carry my passport with me. My checks, personal documents, everything I need. I can leave immediately. Nothing of importance is left in the room. The train station is across the canal. I'll be there right away. I take the first train available, wherever it goes. I aim to travel as far away from Venice as possible, ideally across the border. I will probably cross that border unhindered, now that there may be no one left to plot against me. The infamous diary lies on Van Rijn's corpse, and it will reach its intended destination. Those people will leave me alone. I don't even know who they are.

I had hoped to recognize a pattern and unravel a conspiracy, but that will not happen. This is the nature of conspiracies—that they cannot be unraveled.

And what about London? What awaits me there?

Within a few hours, as soon as Michael's body is found, the Venetian police inform the British consulate. Then the whole machine comes into operation. Foreign Affairs alerts the Metropolitan Police, who in turn informs the family. And who will await me on my return? I won't have anything meaningful to say about this case, especially because I can't be linked to any murder or to Michael's stay in Venice. Everything I did against him disappears from the scene. Master Morse intervenes and guides me through the storm that follows. The media, the police, the court, the family. It will drag on for months, but no one will have anything against me.

And then, within a year or so, I'll be rich enough to take care of my future. The family will want to limit further damage at all costs, and as far as they are concerned, there will not be a lawsuit. Then I disappear. I'm planning to travel abroad, as I find the United Kingdom too intimidating. Maybe Italy; who knows. It is possible to build a future in Italy, although not in Venice.

I wonder what happened to Edvardo. A body has been found, with his documents. There is nothing to indicate that it is actually Edvardo. That he really is dead. If he's able to get a gun into my safe without anyone noticing, he might as well disappear, leaving behind another body. So he escaped, but I'll never hear from him again.

Good for him.

I think he deserves to come out of this unscathed.

Me too, but that's just my own opinion. Not many people will be interested in my opinion.

ACKNOWLEDGMENTS

Special thanks go to Britta Fath and Greet Bauweleers, who critically reviewed the original manuscript, Matthew Rees who carefully edited the text (all the remaining errors are mine), and to Peter Riva (of course), my agent, who makes it all possible.

ABOUT THE AUTHOR

Guido Eekhaut has published crime books, thrillers, and speculative fiction in both Dutch and English. His novel *Absint* (*Absinthe*) won the Hercule Poirot Award, and he has been nominated twice for the Golden Noose Award, as well as the Diamond Bullet. In addition to his Noir series, Eekhaut also writes detective novels under the name Nellie Mandel. He divides his time between Belgium and Spain.

GUIDO EEKHAUT

FROM OPEN ROAD MEDIA

Find a full list of our authors and titles at www.openroadmedia.com

FOLLOW US
@OpenRoadMedia

EARLY BIRD BOOKS

FRESH DEALS, DELIVERED DAILY

Love to read?
Love great sales?

Get fantastic deals on bestselling ebooks delivered to your inbox every day!

Sign up today at
earlybirdbooks.com/book

www.ingramcontent.com/pod-product-compliance
Lightning Source LLC
Chambersburg PA
CBHW031036310726
48969CB00007B/1998